Flutter, Flutter, Butterfly

Age 15. Abused by thousands of soldiers -
Based on a True Story

Mihee Eun

Translated from Korean by Anna Lee

DORRANCE
PUBLISHING CO
EST. 1920
PITTSBURGH, PENNSYLVANIA 15238

The contents of this work, including, but not limited to, the accuracy of events, people, and places depicted; opinions expressed; permission to use previously published materials included; and any advice given or actions advocated are solely the responsibility of the author, who assumes all liability for said work and indemnifies the publisher against any claims stemming from publication of the work.

Dorrance Publishing Co
585 Alpha Drive
Suite 103
Pittsburgh, PA 15238
Visit our website at *www.dorrancebookstore.com*

ISBN: 978-1-4809-4114-4
eISBN: 978-1-4809-4137-3

Contents

Prologue v
1. Flutter, Flutter, Butterfly 1
2. Two Men 5
3. Hiding under the Shadow 9
4. One More Darkness 13
5. Forced to Ride a Truck 17
6. Farewell 23
7. Red-Bricked Building 27
8. Police Station 33
9. Transit Train 39
10. Busan Harbor 45
11. Death of the Girl 51
12. Future, Disappeared 57
13. New Job 61
14. Room 3 67
15. Meeting the Butterfly Again 71
16. A Haircut 75
17. Embittered Life 81
18. Comfort Station, Military Club, Game Room 83
19. Dreams of Death 89
20. Time as an Animal 93
21. Life, Segmented 95
22. Infertile Body 99
23. Secret Conspiracy 103
24. Expanding the Battle Line 107
25. The Legend of a Star 111
26. Condom, Cookies, Blouse 115

27. Conspire to Escape 121
28. Kumok 125
29. Being Arrested 131
30. Back to the Comfort Station 135
31. Choice 139
32. Disappeared Bongnyeo 145
33. Bongnyeo's Missing 149
34. Bongnyeo 151
35. Plan for Revenge 157
36. Chosenpi 161
37. Kumok is Sick 163
38. Farewell, Kumok 167
39. Nightmare Recommenced 171

Prologue

I don't remember my name… I have forgotten. I don't exist anywhere in this world, I am a ghost. But the one name that I can remember now is Haruko – the name that kept haunting me, the name that kept harassing me, the name that I wished to eliminate completely from my life – Haruko.

They gave me this name, Haruko: Chun-Ja, 'a lady of spring.'

Because of this name, my beautiful and cozy spring days have turned to darkness and fallen into hell. The name that represents a dark era, a humiliating life and of living as an animal.

I wish I could delete my shameful past, like an eraser that wipes everything out. I wish I could reset my ruined life and go back to the warm spring field where I chased a butterfly. However, even if I did…I still couldn't remove the name 'Haruko' from my life.

The only reason I recall this name now, though I have always been eager to bury it entirely, is that I don't have much time to live. Wait. No, I am already not in this world. My life is adrift, having cast off the shell of my body… *flutter, flutter, flutter.*

Butterflies are floating in the blue sky. One, two, three…. I know those butterflies – I have wished to be a butterfly, too. Maybe, at this moment, big slithery wings are already growing on my back and sides.

Where am I now? I'm not sure whether I am in this life, or the next life – or on the edge of somewhere.

Those butterflies! What pathetic lives they have!

I accuse the world on behalf of those poor lives and all other pathetically dead lives. I blame the assholes who have destroyed every inch of my life, testifying to their brutalization that viciously tore my flower-like youth into pieces. But please don't shed tears for me. Neither try to mourn for me nor comfort me. Only feel pain and sorrow for the fact that we didn't protect ourselves. Only, be angry that the country did not care about us. Be furious about it.

My excruciating life started at the well. On the road where I was bringing a snack to my parents working in the field. On the path that was once filled with joyfulness, happiness, and excitement for my dreams.

Yet... I met wretchedness on that road. A nightmare flew into my life, along with a fluttering butterfly on this very road.

1. Flutter, Flutter, Butterfly

A softly floating white object arrested Soonboon's eyes. It drifted gently in the wind without sitting in one place and kept flying up and down in the air like paper, a flower petal, an illumination. Soonboon wondered what it was. *Is that a butterfly? Already? It shouldn't be here yet. It is still cold, the wind like the blade of a knife.*

Soonboon's eyes followed the white object, full of curiosity. It danced with big fluttering wings as if catching and releasing the wind. The wings didn't rest for a moment, as though the wind would not allow it, or as if they were being tickled by the spring sun. *Why is it in such a hurry to come out in this cold weather, when the last cold snap has not yet gone away?* she wondered.

The butterfly didn't stay in one place patiently fluttering its wings. With the death of the cocoon came the wings that allow it to float without ceasing. *Flutter, flutter, flutter…*

"Butterfly, butterfly! Come here. I am going to catch you to show my mom!" Soonboon stretched out her arms to grab the butterfly, but it was not to be caught easily. Tantalizingly, the butterfly flew as if it might be caught or barely escape Soonboon's reach. Just a little farther, a couple of steps ahead, like playing hide and seek, the butterfly led her, teased her. Soonboon might have given up if it had flown far away, but the butterfly maintained a close distance, keeping her attention.

In fact, Soonboon didn't want to catch the butterfly. If she had really wanted to grab it, she could have, but she didn't. She preferred to let it float with its delicate wings wherever it wanted to go since, like other creatures, it had only come out into the world to survive.

Soonboon thought back on this time last year when her sister got married, and the butterflies had just started to come out into the world. Most daughters of wealthy families were led into their wedding banquets by a decorated red and blue candle, riding on a colorful palanquin, wearing rouge on their cheeks and foreheads, wearing beautiful dresses. But her sister got married without rouge on her cheeks and forehead and without a beautiful dress. Yet her dad wanted to show his love, so he prepared a comforter set to send to the bride's new house with all the money he had saved over the years.

"Be happy, be loved by your husband and respect your in-laws."

With these words, Soonboon's mom sent off her daughter, wiping away her tears with the hem of her skirt. Her sister cried happily as she left the house. She was a little nervous about leaving the nest and entering a new world, but she was also excited. A shy smile lighted her tear-covered face. *I will do the same thing one day. I will get married like my sister did. Right when the butterflies start to float, right when they first come out into the world. The season when forsythia, azalea, cornelian cherry flower, ginger lily, magnolia, and wild roses show their faces. When that happens, I will go far away and begin a new life.* Soonboon's heart beat with expectation and excitement at that thought.

One day, there would be talk of her marriage. Who would be her husband? Sooner or later, she would probably marry a complete stranger, have babies, and get older, just like her mom and sister did. Starting her new life as a radiant bride, she would raise her children, and then grow old like a good grandmother does, lead an ordinary life, and be scattered in the end, a handful of ashes. That's the life she wished to live, and that's the life her parents wanted for her. It's the life most people wish to live.

Soonboon started to chase the butterfly again. It had been sitting on a branch that looked like it would sprout soon, and then suddenly it flew up. It hovered around her as if it was telling her to catch it if she could. She tenderly approached the butterfly and stretched her arms out to grab it.

"I got you, you little wretch!" But the butterfly was still too fast for Soonboon's hands. It flew right through the space between her fingers and out of her grasp. Soonboon envied its bright, smooth wings that could glide through the air. If she had those wings, she could go anywhere she wanted. Since the day she was born, Soonboon had never left her hometown. She had only heard stories about the world beyond her hometown from peddlers. She collected their stories and imagined other worlds; that was all she knew. The world, she believed, was full of excitement and trembling. She waited until she would get married, and finally be carried away from her birthplace. Her parents would send her off with tears in their eyes, and she would move somewhere far away in another world.

At that moment, Soonboon stopped walking. She tilted her chin up and took a deep breath of the spring air. The sunlight rushed into her body. Absorbing the spring sunshine, her body began to itch. The feeling of spring circulated in her blood and tickled her body with a desire to grow wings. Soonboon started to dance. The butterfly danced above her.

Soonboon felt wings growing on her back- dazzling white ones just like the butterfly's. She felt as if she could fly if she flapped her arms hard enough. There was a tingling in the soles of her feet. Particles of wind and sunshine kissed her softly, inciting her: fly, fly, fly. She heard a whisper in her ears. Was it the wind or the butterfly? *Fly, fly.* The whisper was sweet like a secret, and she felt like she could take off if she stretched out her arms. Her feet were already off the ground.

Suddenly, she was afraid she would get lost while she flew. She was fearful that she might lose her parents and she wouldn't be able to find her house again. It was not the right time, not yet. *Later, I will fly away, encouraged by my parents. I will get married and grow older like my mom, have babies and watch them grow.* Soonboon wondered who her husband would be. She didn't have any man in her heart, no one who was worth it. She would obey her parents' matchmaking, and that would be it.

"You will eventually learn how to live with affection," her mother answered simply when Soonboon asked her how she felt the first time she was intimate with her husband. Mom turned her head to the left, feeling water vapors on her face as she poured barley out from the big cast iron pot.

"Did you like dad when you first met him? How did you feel? How did you like him?" Soonboon asked as her mom scratched the bottom of the pot, using the large bowl to scrape everything out. Her mom replied:

"I didn't have any feeling about whether I liked him or not. I just felt what he was."

"But that's no fun at all. Didn't you have any lovers when you were younger?"

"Move away from the stove, you might get burned," her mom interrupted, moving the boiled barley instead of answering.

"You will eventually learn how to live with affection," mom told her sister also, when she got married. "There is nothing special about women's lives," she said. "The best thing you can do is to meet a nice husband. There is nothing better than that. Then there are three rules: be obedient to your father when you are young, be loyal to your husband once you are married, and listen to your son after your husband has died. This is the highest virtue you can have as a woman. A woman's life is to stay under the shade of men. Be obedient to your husband and dedicate yourself to him. Everything will be okay if he doesn't cheat on you or abuse you. The next important thing is that you have three meals a day without starving."

Her sister quietly nodded. Soonboon became full of curiosity as to whom her shade would be.

2. Two Men

At that moment, two men came from the direction where the butterfly had flown away. One man was wearing a camouflage military uniform, and the other, middle-aged, was wearing a white shirt with black pants. Both were short. Soonboon was terrified by the long sword on the soldier's waist. She had a sudden gut feeling that she was their target. She turned away as if she suddenly realized something that she had to do.

"Hey, hey," they called her as she turned. She walked fast as if to get away. "Hey."

They called again. Soonboon walked faster. Needless to say, the men's strides were broader and quicker than hers, and the distance between them got smaller. She must run away, she must disappear from their sight. She could get into big trouble if she was caught. Horrific rumors had filled people's minds with fear in this wartime. Soonboon did not want to be the main character in one of those horrible stories.

"Stop there."

The voice became fiercer and more abrupt.

She might be caught in their net. Then, everything would be over. 'virgin delivery,' they had called it: the story of the Japanese army recruiting virgins and delivering them to the army in the battlefield. Teenage girls and unmarried women, what would the army do with naïve young girls who had holiness in their bodies, like prohibited land? If girls hadn't yet reached a certain age, the Japanese would measure their weight and force them to join the recruitment. If parents tried to hide them, soldiers would rummage through the houses.

Girls of the colony were treated by the Japanese like commodities to be sold: rice, salt, or cotton. Even some men were taken, to be used as human shields on the battlefield or sent to do compulsory labor: building roads, making tunnels, or constructing airports. These men did work that oxen should do, that horses have to do, that plows ought to do.

Colonial people like Soonboon were not seen as human beings to the Japanese. Their lives were like blades of grass, mowed down and ends strewn away. These people often abandoned their ancestral names and were forced by the Japanese not to use their mother tongues. They were told to throw away their spirits. Their lands were taken, no longer theirs though these were where they were born. Nothing could be done of their own will. Therefore, the only solution to survive under the Japanese oppression was to live like invisible men and women. They could not cast their own shadows; they had to hide all evidence of mere existence.

"Don't go outside. Be careful no one notices you. The world is chaotic, and I want you to get married soon, but I am worried since there are no bachelors. They have all been sent to battlefields or construction sites. I secretly asked a matchmaker for help, but I'm not sure that will make a difference. We have to hurry to find you a husband, if we can, but in the meantime, make sure you don't hang around outside. You should be fine as long as no one sees you."

Soonboon remembered now what her dad had said a few days ago. After having dinner, in the middle of a dark night, dad had expressed this tiredly, letting out a deep sigh. Mom also took a deep and painful sigh, sitting next to dad.

"They have been searching every house for unmarried women. They might have heard about you already. So you must hide as if you don't live here. Do not forget."

Dad reminded her of this over and over. She should have been more careful. But she didn't listen. She should have stayed inside, undetectable, but she was noticed while she was out chasing butterflies. Soonboon ran with all her strength away from the two men. The butterfly that had flown away now followed her, as if it had never left. Soonboon ran, and the butterfly flew, alternating who was ahead and who was behind. But Soonboon did not notice the butterfly this time. She was too busy running with all her strength, holding her breath.

Spring sunshine had spread widely in all directions. The wind mixed with the sunshine, scattering the dirt flying up from the road. She couldn't open her eyes because the dust blocked her vision, and the mixture kept entering her mouth. She chewed the dust in her mouth. The distance between Soonboon and the men was getting smaller still. She jumped down to the slope on the side of the road. She knew of a small hole in the middle of the hill that she could hide in. It was just big enough to conceal a young girl. Nobody from the outside could see her if she hid inside the hole. Soonboon crawled inside. Sharp stones poked her palms, but she didn't feel any pain. When she held her breath, she heard the sound of men's footsteps, *rat-a-tat-tat*. Then the sound stopped.

"Where has she gone? She was supposed to be here. That little scamp."

Through the hole, she could see the soldier's boots with military gaiters. If she took a big breath, they would hear her. They were hanging around the hole instead of continuing on.

"What a little capricious bitch," the soldier growled, kicking the ground with rage.

"Let's go. I know whose daughter she is. We can come back tomorrow and take her. Let's go back now."

Does he know me? Then who is he? Soonboon wondered.

How much time has passed? Finally, the men went off to where they had started. Soonboon held her breath until they had completely disappeared. Suddenly, she remembered the butterfly.

Butterfly. Where is the butterfly? She looked for the butterfly, her body crouched low like a caterpillar. The butterfly had been right ahead of her before she hid in the hole. But where had it gone? *Butterfly, butterfly! Where are you now?*

After the men disappeared, as the sun's shadow grew, Soonboon came out from the hole. She felt stiff as a wooden log since she hadn't stretched her body for several hours. Releasing her bent joints, she felt her blood begin to re-circulate her body. She left before the shadows got any longer.

3. Hiding under the Shadow

Far away, mom and dad could be seen bending their backs to pick up stones, and pulling weeds from among the barley crop. Her parents looked like small shrubs with loosened branches that don't produce leaves anymore. Like goats, skinny from starvation.

"Mom, mom…" Her words broke due to her shortness of breath. With every exhalation, her words slipped away.

"Dad."

"What happened? Why are you in such a hurry? Did you see a ghost in the middle of the day?" Mom asked, picking grass from the barley field, sensing something unusual in her daughter's steps.

Dad looked at Soonboon.

"A soldier, I saw a soldier. He called to me, so I ran away quickly."

"What? A soldier? Called to you?"

Dad straightened his back in shock.

"Yes."

"Oh my god. Oh my god. We are in big trouble now. Little girl, I told you to stay at home. What should we do?"

"I just wanted to bring you some snacks."

She suddenly remembered the potatoes and water kettle she had forgotten while playing with the butterfly.

"Are you crazy? You're out of your mind. Who said that you needed to bring a snack for us? I told you should stay home, and not to go outside." Mom hit Soonboon's back with a thick hand, sending Soonboon to the brink of tears in pain.

"What should we do? What should we do now?"

"Go home with Soonboon now to avoid any mishaps," dad said with a gruff voice and took the hoe from mom's hand. She was nervous and in a hurry to get Soonboon home. Dad's face was full of wrinkles and psoriasis. Mom took off her headscarf and dusted it off on her clothes, then covered up her head with it like a hood. She grabbed her daughter's wrist abruptly and dragged her down the slope of the mountain path. Soonboon knew that mom had chosen this road instead of the plain one to prevent them from being seen.

"We should have married you off by now. Then we would not be in this trouble. What should we do? What should we do? This is serious. We are in serious trouble."

Mom scurried along the rough road, her buttocks covered by her long skirt shaking. Soonboon giggled quietly at the sight of her mom's dancing backside in the middle of the mountain road.

"You, crazy little girl! How can you laugh in such a grave situation?"

Mom turned around suddenly and scolded her daughter. Soonboon stopped giggling, embarrassed.

"You, immature girl! Didn't you hear the news? Ilryung, your neighbor, was taken. She was dragged somewhere for virgin delivery coming back from the well with a pail of water. And it's not just Ilryung; the whole town is in turmoil."

Soonboon knew Ilryung well. She was two years older than Soonboon. They ran into each other sometimes in a narrow alley or on the side of a stream. Soonboon knew it hadn't only happened to Ilryung. Her neighbor Youngsoon been married at a young age to avoid the virgin delivery. Okja left the town riding on a truck bed because she hadn't been able to evade it. Other familiar girls hadn't shown up at the well for some time. They didn't get married, they didn't go to babysit the rich, and they didn't go off to be maidservants either, as some of them were told. Someone said that they left for a factory to make money or someone else stated that they went off for their studies, but nobody believed it. Nobody knew what happened to the girls or where they had gone. Parents kept their mouths shut, shaking their heads as if they knew nothing. But terrible news disturbed the people's ears and hearts.

Soonboon kept slipping as she tried to keep up with mom. Sometimes, she took false steps as if she were tripping over imaginary holes, and other times she fell to the ground for stepping in the wrong place.

"What are you doing? Stay focused."

Mom felt uncomfortable about her daughter's awkward behavior. Soonboon became depressed. She didn't want to fall down, either. She felt like something was reaching up and grabbing her ankles from deep within the ground. But before long, her depression softened like an ice-cream melting in the sunlight. She was sorry that she hadn't listened to her father's biddings.

Soonboon and her parents were barely able to survive off of their farming, and mom was always hungry. They had nothing left to eat even after a harvest in the fall. A landowner took half of the crop, and the government deprived the rest of it as an enormous quota. They begged and fought against their harvest being taken for fear that they would starve to death, but it was no use. It was possible that they would get hurt if they resisted. Even if they tried to hide the harvest where nobody could see it, it was futile. Police and spies were everywhere: they were in the sky, on the ground and even beside them.

Tenant farmers like her parents tilled the land all year round like ants, but they were barely allowed to keep enough grain to prevent them from starving. They would have to survive on those few grains until next year. They boiled grass roots and tree bark and ate them to relieve their empty stomachs. At times, they hardly managed to stay alive. But life was tenacious. They survived the winter, their faces yellowish and swollen from starvation, and they tolerated their springtime hunger. Although they often wished they were dead, they didn't die.

Dad complained that he'd rather live off herb roots and tree bark rather than succumb to the loss of a harvest that he had made with his own sweat. Nevertheless, he plowed the land and sowed crops in the field each spring because he felt such anticipation and eagerness to do so- that was the life of a tenant farmer.

Soonboon suddenly stopped and looked back at the road they had passed as she was dragged by her mom by the wrist. "Mom, wait a second. I forgot to take the potato basket while I was running away. I need to find the basket."

"You stupid little girl, are you still insane? Is that important right now in this situation where you might be taken away?"

Not important? Food, food meant everything to them. Meaningless? Soonboon had always been scared of someone taking the grains, so she hid them carefully. For how long had she been scared, hiding potatoes to relieve their hunger? The potatoes were her family's lifeline.

"It won't take long..."

"This immature girl! What if somebody notices you?"

"It's not far from here. I can be done quick."

"Oh my god, stupid girl! You still don't understand how serious this situation is even though I told you so many times. Wake up, little girl!"

Mom pulled Soonboon's wrist so hard that Soonboon almost fell down. It was such a shame that she had forgotten the potatoes. *I should have held them as I ran away. I might not have forgotten the potatoes if I hadn't been crazy enough to chase that butterfly.* When they reached a narrow alley after coming down the mountain slope, her mother walked faster. Her steps were faster than usual. She couldn't trust or believe anyone. Arriving home, mom pushed aside some bundles of straw near the kitchen and pointed in between them.

"Hide here. Do not come out even if somebody calls you. From now on, you do not live in this house. Do you understand? You don't exist anymore. Do not come out although your dad or I call your name. Stay inside of this straw bundle. I will give you a chamber pot that you can pee in. Never come out. You got it?" mom threatened. Thick darkness permeated inside the haystack. There was only a small space for one person to sit. Soonboon was hesitant- the space looked like a tomb.

"Why don't you go inside?"

Mom hurried her up. Soonboon reluctantly hid herself in the darkness. Mom covered her with more straw after she got inside. Dust tickled her nose when she breathed, causing her to sneeze: *achoo, achoo. Tap-tap*, mom touched the straws with her hands. It was a signal that she should not sneeze. She stopped herself from sneezing. *How long will I have to stay here? One day? Two days? One month?* She didn't have any idea how long it would be.

4. One More Darkness

"Soonboon, Soonboon!"

Soonboon had fallen asleep. She raised her head at the sound of her name. Then, *ouch*, she groaned. A sharp pain halted her breath, and she felt like a sword was cutting her joints. She tried to straighten her legs, neck, arms, and waist, but she was not comfortable enough to move. Whenever she moved, something scratched the back of her hand, or she bumped into something. *Where am I?* A narrow and confined space. She was not in her room since she couldn't see her door covered with cross-patterned paper. There was only darkness there, instead of dusky light. Slowly, Soonboon realized that she was still inside the haystack. *Right, that's right. I am hiding inside the haystacks.* She must have fallen asleep unwittingly. After realizing this, she was relieved from the sudden fear, and she dispelled the heavy sleepiness by rolling her stiff joints.

She didn't dream, for the narrow and confined space would not allow her to dream. Instead, endless silence overtook her. The silence was a loneliness whose cause was unknown. Not knowing the future gave her a fear whose depth she could not fathom. The silence consumed her. *What time is it?* She wondered. But time was meaningless in the haystack.

"Soonboon, Soonboon."

It was coming from behind the straw bundle: mom. The low voice in the silence sounded like soft wind.

"Come out, come out and let's go to sleep," mom called to her, delicately. Soonboon came out, dispersing the straw around her. The dust hovered, coming again into her nose and mouth. She sneezed again.

Achoo.

"Baby, why are you not being careful?"

Mom was surprised at her sneezing and covered Soonboon's face with her skirt. But Soonboon kept sneezing, not answering her question. *Achoo!* The sneeze was loud as a scream, and it was making a short echo in the darkness. *ACHOO!*

"Oh no, baby."

Mom was embarrassed by her constant sneezing. Milky-colored snot dangled at the end of Soonboon's nose. She wiped her runny nose with her right sleeve and spit out the mucus on the ground. Soonboon could smell the sweat from her mom's underwear. It was the scent of life, the scent of a mom.

"You'd better sleep in comfort. Let's go to the room. Hide again tomorrow before sunrise."

Soonboon's movement from darkness to darkness was cautious so as not to be discovered. She followed her mom, bending her back, almost crawling on the ground. She was good at moving in the darkness without any light. Mom and Soonboon groped around in the dark and got underneath the comforter. Dad moved closer to the wall to make space for his wife and daughter.

"Sleep, and you'll go back into the straw bundle tomorrow early in the morning." Mom whispered, believing that the walls had ears. Soonboon attempted to clear her throat. She could smell a mixture of her dad's sweat and her mom's flesh. The unknowns of tomorrow made the quiet darkness sad.

"We need to find a bridegroom for you. A widower would be fine…"

Dad spat the words out in a sigh, and mom didn't say anything back. Instead, she stroked the back of Soonboon's hand.

"Even animals don't choose mates of another age."

He lay on his side instead of responding. Mom's hand trembled slightly.

'Virgin delivery.' What do they do after taking the virgins? Do they send them off to be babysitters or nurses to take care of wounded soldiers on the battlefield? Her thoughts circled over and over again, and she finally fell asleep at the end of her maze-like thoughts. Healthy bodies require more sleep, but sleep felt like death for her.

How long had she slept? Someone awakened Soonboon, but she couldn't open her eyes. The touch of a tough hand forced her awake eventually.

"Go and hide. It is morning."

Soonboon looked around with sleepy eyes, and she noticed that twilight was reflecting off the mulberry paper-covered door, and then she remembered the situation. It was time to hide again in the grave-like pile of straw. She slowly moved to get into the straw with half-opened eyes. Not to be detected, Soonboon should turn into a straw and should become in harmony with the darkness.

"Whoever calls you, never come out!"

Mom said earnestly. Soonboon dug herself a space in the pile of dust-filled straw. She curled her body like a worm and held her breath to turn into the darkness. She couldn't do anything inside there except doze. She dozed and dozed, but still it seemed the time would not pass. No, it seemed as if time had frozen.

Suddenly, she felt something hovering over her head. She opened her eyes and saw a butterfly fluttering there. At first, Soonboon doubted what she saw, but it was surely the white butterfly. How could it be there with her in the darkness? No, how could it enter into the straw? The butterfly floated among the pieces of straw which now resembled insect nets. *No way.* At that moment, Soonboon forgot what mom had said. She was captivated by the butterfly. Despite mom's strong urging to never come out, Soonboon climbed out of the haystack and went out through the kitchen door, not knowing who would be waiting for her in the bright sunlight.

5. Forced to Ride a Truck

Soonboon could barely see anything, having come so quickly out from the darkness. She closed her eyes involuntarily. How long had she been standing there? As she blocked the sun's dazzling light with her hands, she noticed two men in front of her, laughing at her.

"Who… who are you?"

Soonboon asked, moving back by instinct. One man was wearing a light tan and bright green uniform, the other was a village leader.

"Gotcha, you little ratch! Didn't you know we could find you even if you were hiding like a rat?"

The soldier's voice sounded metallic. Soonboon was too afraid to take a breath.

"How old are you?" the soldier with an oily face asked Soonboon.

Soonboon took a step back as he came a step closer, and she moved two steps back when he got two steps closer. But the soldier's stride was longer than Soonboon's, and the space between them diminished. If he stretched out his arms, he could grab her by the wrist. Soonboon thought to run, but she couldn't move, she couldn't lift her legs from the ground. She stared at the two men without moving at all like a tree root buried deep in the soil. *You should hide, not to be detected by anyone, you must not come out no matter what happens.* She remembered what her dad had said. She must flee, she must run away from them like the butterfly that slipped through the cracks in her hands. She put all her strength into her legs, but something heavy grabbed her neck as she was about to step forward. It felt like a hook or a barbed wire. Cold, wiry hands clawed her neck.

"You little bitch. Where are you trying to run away to?"

She was trying to resist and was struggling against him, but she couldn't get out of his grip. The more she stumbled, the firmer the hands grabbed her neck. *Rip*, went the sound of her *jeogori*[1] being cut. Soonboon couldn't resist the power.

"Let me go, please, let me go," Soonboon begged, suffocating.

"Do you think you can escape? Bitch, don't you know it's useless to run away?"

The soldier with the short-brimmed hat spoke, and the village leader watched. The soldier's strong hands came down from her neck and grabbed her arm.

"Please, let me go." Soonboon flailed her arms and tried to get out from the soldier's grasp. But the more she waved her arms, the more the soldier's hands tightened.

"It hurts, it hurts." Soonboon tried pulling the soldier's hand off with her other hand, but it was useless. The butterfly was nowhere to be seen. *Was it really a butterfly? Did I see a ghost instead?*

"If you rebel against the command of the Great Japanese Emperor, you will only meet death." The soldier's words drained all the power from her body. As he felt Soonboon's resistance subside, he released the arm he had gripped so tightly.

"Listen carefully to what I say. Is there an adult in the house?"

The soldier asked, catching a glimpse of the room, but the door was closed. Mom and dad had gone to the field right after sunrise. They worked hard to survive; nevertheless, their lives were still impoverished. Despite working from early morning until night without once stretching their backs, their lives had not gotten any better. In spite of having good harvests in the fall, they still barely had a couple of handfuls of rice for themselves. They could not dream of the future.

"Nobody is at home."

Ignoring Soonboon, he approached the master bedroom and prowled around.

"Hmmm…" After he had made sure nobody was at home, he looked back at Soonboon with a sinister laugh.

"You! Do you want to make money?"

The poisoned and cold attitude he had just moments ago had disappeared. His voice had delicate tones now. *Money?* Soonboon asked with her eyes.

[1] A basic upper garment of hanbok, Korean traditional garment

"You'll make money, depending on how you behave of course. How about that? Do you want to make money?"

The soft voice triggered Soonboon's curiosity.

"Money?" Soonboon felt strange although she was curious.

"Yes, money, a lot of money."

When Soonboon showed interest, the soldier spoke gently with a smile on his lips:

"You can make large amounts of money if you make up your mind to come with us. We are going to an airplane factory in Japan. You will get a salary every month. Lots of your friends have already gone there to make money. You will see them if you come with us."

"I can make a lot of money?" Soonboon asked again. The soldier with the short-brimmed hat and smiling eyes told her yes.

"How old are you?"

He glanced up and down at Soonboon's body.

"Fifteen... I'm fifteen years old," Soonboon replied immediately.

Soonboon's mind was busy. She didn't want to miss the chance to help her family, and she was afraid now that they might leave without taking her.

"Fifteen years old. Hmmm…"

The soldier walked around Soonboon, checking her physique carefully. He was pleased about Soonboon's round-shaped face, flat nose, and her chubby little white-skinned body.

"You look good. *Yoi*, let's go." The soldier nodded his head as if he was satisfied with her.

Soonboon had lots of things she could do with the money. First, she wished to buy her family's land for her dad. His whole life had been attached to that land like all tenant farmers. She yearned to give him an area that was officially his where he could work until he died. Soonboon wanted him to gain self-esteem and to feel the joy of having a real harvest, something he'd never had. The land itself was fertilized by an accumulation of his sweat, efforts, and sighs; he deserved to have it in his name.

In the spring, brilliant sunshine pooled abundantly in the fields, blue waves rolled in during the summer, and the fields turned golden-yellow in the fall. Dad valued that land as more precious than his own life. His own body led him out into the fields each spring, though nobody forced him to. His hands suffered from frost-bite, his cheeks were chapped from harsh winds, and his back got more and more crooked every year. But his heart filled with happiness when he looked at the land.

Mihee Eun

Soonboon wanted to bury her parents' bodies at a corner of the property when they died. She wanted to build an eternal house for them on that land. She was proud of herself for having this idea. It was enough if her parents could be happy, even if she might have to suffer from hard work.

"Did you say airplane factory? Will they really give me a salary?"

"Yes, absolutely. It is not hard work, either. You can also go to school if you like. You can work during the day and study at night. It depends on how you want to do it. What do you think? Do you want to go?"

"Are you sure?"

"Yes, of course."

"Really?"

Soonboon asked for confirmation again. Every time she asked, the soldier answered with a gentle face that reminded her of her dad. He was urging her to go with them, subtly now. Soonboon looked back toward the village leader. He held her gaze and nodded his head.

"It is not hard work, you just need to assemble airplane parts."

"Okay, I will go."

With her answer, Soonboon felt a strong energy rush through her body with a type of joy.

The soil under the blush-clover fence was slightly swollen, black, and fertile. *Dad will sprinkle balsam seeds in there when I am gone. Then balsam flowers will brighten the house for the season, and after that, they will wither away.*

Dad liked flowers. Soonboon never understood how such soft emotions could exist in a man's heart. But every spring, dad sprinkled balsam seeds without fail. Each time he sprinkled the seeds, which looked like black perilla seeds, he was afraid that the magpies would eat them, so he carefully covered them with soil. His hair grayed and his hands grew rough from tilling the land. Still, he knelt down every year under the fence in the bright pool of sunshine, holding a hoe in one hand and the balsam seeds in the other. Once he was close to the wall, he dug up the frozen winter soil. He turned the soil over gently with his hands and the particles spread like flower petals under his fingertips. Mom would look at dad with a sideways glance and scold him in a loud voice:

"If you have enough time to sprinkle balsam seeds, you'd just as well sleep more. Do you really have time for flowers? Life is tough."

But Soonboon didn't sense displeasure in her mom's voice. Watching dad do this, mom's eyes were soft with affection. Dad didn't care much about mom's scolding, he just thought about the balsam flowers that would bloom under the fence all summer. Soonboon liked that he did. As the sunshine warmed the shade and the cozy spring haze rose, Soonboon watched her dad sprinkling the seeds with sleepy eyes. When the black seeds sprouted, revealing white and red petals, Soonboon would dye her fingernails with them and collected the seeds for next year.

After the balsam flowers had bloomed four times, Soonboon would come back. And after that, she would get married. *I will have a wedding ceremony with rouge on my cheeks and forehead, wearing a blue jeogori and a red skirt. Then I will move to a new world riding on a colorfully decorated palanquin.*

"I will leave tomorrow after talking to my parents tonight."

Soonboon answered, feeling like an adult.

"No, we don't have time. We need to leave right now. If you don't come with us now, somebody else will take your place," the village leader said, reading the soldier's face.

"I need to ask my parents first," said Soonboon, embarrassed now.

"There's no time for that. The truck is ready. You cannot be late." His voice had turned threatening. All sweetness had disappeared from the soldier's face. Instead, he was intimidating and fierce. His eyes were vicious in the shade of his hat and made her tremble.

"I can't leave like this."

Soonboon replied, taking a step back. She was planning on plunging into her room and locking the door if he kept insisting. But they were faster than her. The soldier's glaring eyes were as intense as though they were touching her face.

"Why are you doing this?" Soonboon stepped back, pushing him.

"If you don't listen when I am talking to you nicely, then fine."

Soonboon realized that something was off by his sudden change in attitude. She felt dizzy. Something was wrong. The village leader's hands grasped her immediately and threw her into the truck without giving her a moment to react. It was as though he was catching a rabbit. She resisted, saying she didn't want to go. She begged them to let her go, but it was useless. It was already over.

Soonboon always thought the idea of virgin delivery was just a rumor. She never imagined it would come true for her. Until now, she had believed that unpleasant things only happened to others. Soonboon kept looking back over her shoulder as she rode forward on the truck bed. She felt like a bale of hay tossed on the ground.

From a distance, the house looked like an old, sleepy beast, the afternoon sun hanging low on the roof like a blanket. The light was too bright for Soonboon to stare any longer.

I will come back, surely I will. When balsam flowers bloom four times, I will certainly come back. But will I really? Soonboon's eyes were getting wet with tears. This was the hometown that she had never left since she was born. How would her parents react when they found out their daughter was missing? *Never go outside. You don't exist in this house anymore. Be careful, don't let anyone even see your shadow.* They had warned her, and she had disobeyed them. She was riddled with guilt now that she hadn't followed their advice yet again.

6. Farewell

Two girls were crouched in the back of the truck Soonboon was thrown in. They were very young. One girl's *jeogori* string was torn, and her bruised eye made it apparent that she had tried to fight back before being thrown into the truck. The other girl was short, cute, and had a chubby face. The two girls stared at Soonboon. Then they moved their bottoms aside and made a space for her.

One girl looked at Soonboon with swollen eyes. Soonboon didn't know how they had been taken, but she was relieved not to be alone. Maybe they shared the same fears, and maybe they'd open their hearts to her.

Right after Soonboon was hurled in the truck, it started to rumble, boisterously spitting out exhaust. The truck bed shook from the bumpy country roads, and the girls had to hold on to the bar so as not to fall off entirely. Their bottoms tingled with pain from all the shaking. Soonboon squinted to avoid the wind but the invisible wind was so strong that it scratched their faces and blocked their breathing. Soonboon shut her mouths and closed her eyes. As she looked back at her village getting farther and farther away, Soonboon's eyes moistened. Clouds of dust filled the road and enveloped the village; Soonboon could no longer see the home she'd left and the parents she hadn't said goodbye to. Sadness weighed heavily on her heart.

Soonboon looked down under the truck bed. *What if I jump down from here? Can I?* It seemed impossible to jump from a moving vehicle, at a distance that was taller than herself. As she kept looking down, the land whooshing by made her feel dizzy.

"Where are we going?" the girl with the bruised eye asked, as if talking to herself.

"They said we will go to a factory that makes airplane parts," Soonboon answered. Perhaps what she really wanted was to find out if they had told her the truth.

"Really? They told me I would get to be a nurse," the other girl answered.

Soonboon was confused. Going to an airplane factory or being a nurse? Which was correct?

"How about you? What did they say to you?" Soonboon asked the other girl, but she didn't hear Soonboon's question. She was absorbed in her own thoughts.

"How far is it from here to Japan? I heard it takes several days by ship…" the short, chubby girl murmured. The girls didn't know each other's names but were already worried about what would happen to each other.

"My name is Kumok," again, the same girl spoke her name, looking back and forth between Soonboon and the other girl.

"I am Soonboon, Soonboon," Soonboon answered quickly.

The other girl's name was Bongnyeo. She had broad strong shoulders for her age and clean-cut features that matched her good physique.

"Is it true that we can make money where we are going?" Soonboon asked, now doubting everything the soldier had said.

Kumok answered her, "I have no idea. I was caught while coming back from a friend's house."

"How come?"

"My friend Bobae's dad fetched water at a Japanese house. I went to her house on that day. We met every day because we were very close. When I was on the way back home, suddenly, a Korean with khaki-colored pants and a Japanese soldier wanted to see me for a second. I didn't know why. Mom told me to be careful of virgin delivery, but I didn't know what it was."

Kumok continued telling them how she was caught:

"They brought me somewhere, the road was for Japanese people only. Then, they imprisoned me inside a house. It was a two-story building with a *tatami*[2] floor. I spent three nights there, and then I was put on this truck. They told me that I would be taken to get a job as a nurse. My parents might be crazy enough to search for me since they have no idea whether I am dead or alive after leaving the house." Kumok let out a deep sigh.

[2] a type of mat used as a flooring material in traditional Japanese-style rooms

"I was caught while I was hiding. I was told I could make money at an airplane factory. So... how about you? How were you taken here?" Soonboon asked Bongnyeo. But she still did not respond. She seemed stubborn, or smart, or perhaps both.

The truck drove on for many hours, bouncing along the crooked road. In the meantime, they stopped by a few more villages and peeked around the houses. Birds, wind and a solitary skinny dog were the only apparent owners of these homes. The dog didn't bark when he saw the soldier with a sword on his waist. When the soldier and village leader entered the house, the dog tucked his tail down between his legs, and backed up, looking sheepishly into the men's eyes. They opened a mulberry paper door with several holes, but only stillness existed inside. They searched the backyard, opened the toilet, but they encountered nothing. The village leader blocked one nostril and blew his nose.

"Where have all the girls gone? Ungrateful bitches!"

The soldier knitted his brows and turned back again to where he had just been, confirming that nobody was there. Once they got back in the truck, it started rattling again, breathing roughly like a cranky old man.

"They might be looking around to catch more unmarried women," Kumok said. Her words made Soonboon uneasy.

Why do they take unmarried women? Soonboon's unresolved thoughts made her heart heavy. In the distance Soonboon could see a vivid red-bricked building standing out amongst old, broken houses and stores. As they saw the building, somehow Soonboon and the other girls realized that they wouldn't be going back home.

7. Red-Bricked Building

It was a police station, filled with bone-chilling air. Soonboon and the other girls were put into a small square corner room with a tiny window near the ceiling. The girls sat near the wall, holding their knees. Their thin cotton clothes were not enough to fight the cold coming off the cement wall. Soonboon got goosebumps. Kumok crossed her arms and rubbed them.

Soonboon looked around in every direction, but she couldn't find anything they could use to stay warm. She could see the sun setting through the small window. It was the time of day when all the birds returned to their nests with food for their young. Strangely, the twilight doubled Soonboon's fears and triggered her sadness. Around this time, mom and dad might have noticed that Soonboon was missing. They might be looking for her frantically, turning over the straw bundles again and again where she was supposed to be hiding, not believing that their daughter was gone. But their efforts looking for a trace of their girl would be in vain.

Bongnyeo and Kumok buried their faces between their knees. They raised their heads to stare blankly ahead and hid their faces again. Bongnyeo's eyes were red around the edges as if she might have been beaten. Looking closely, it seemed there was a swelling near her mouth, too. This made Soonboon more afraid than she had been.

Groan! mumbled Bongnyeo. She finally let out a moan after having kept her mouth shut for so many long hours.

"Are you sick?" Soonboon asked with a worried face, but Bongnyeo shook her head, and though she denied it, the grimace on her face told otherwise.

"Lean on my shoulder."

Soonboon brought her shoulder closer to Bongnyeo, hoping she would lean her head on her shoulder. She looked at Soonboon and fixed her posture, smiling reluctantly. She straightened her back, pulled her knees against her chest, and buried her face between her knees. Despite her smile, it seemed like she was crying. Her fake smile weighed on Soonboon's mind. Kumok leaned her head on Soonboon's shoulder instead of Bongnyeo.

"I want to go home. What are my mom and family members doing now?" Kumok spoke to herself.

"So do I. Can we go back home?" Soonboon asked, but Kumok didn't answer this time. Instead of answering, she was drawing something on the floor, and Bongnyeo didn't move at all, her face buried between her knees. What was going to happen to them? *I should have stayed inside, I should have stayed inside the haystacks like mom said. Why did I come out, why?*

Everybody was busy at the police station. The phone rang starkly and a man in a uniform answered it, his posture upright, yelling periodically. A small lightbulb covered by a lampshade hung down near the desk, and there was one bookshelf and one door in the room. Soonboon had never thought she would be in a police station. The words 'police station' had always numbed her with fear.

Soonboon could see a truck pulling up to the police station through the slightly opened door. The truck looked big and sturdy compared to the vehicle she rode. It seemed to stop, and she could suddenly hear bad words.

"Hurry up, why don't you move? Come on, faster, you *Chosenjin*[3], sons of bitches."

Soonboon craned her neck and looked out at the truck. A military policeman banged on the truck and forced the people inside to jump down. At that sound, the men in the truck bed jumped down from all sides. As they were poorly dressed, they must have been caught while they were working in the fields. Perhaps they were taken while tilling the fields, some while walking the road, or at home.

"What happened?" Kumok asked, scooting closer to Soonboon.

"I don't know."

"They might have been taken, like us."

Soonboon remembered that there were young labor workers often captured young men. Soldiers hung around the villages, dragging them away.

[3] Koreans. Japanese word calling Koreans inferior.

After being taken, the young people were sent to factories to construct tunnels, or they were taken to the battlefield. They never returned home; they were taken to become human shields and expendables.

"Are you guys all dipshits? Why don't you hurry, you stupid, lazy bastards!"

The military policeman walked around the men as they jumped down from the truck and kicked them. *Thwack! Thwack!* Some men curled up on the floor or knelt down, holding their harshly kicked abdomens.

"Move faster, you piece of shit!"

The men were forced into a corner, following orders as if they were being hunted. They all seemed terrified, and they were very skinny, wearing seedy clothes. Soonboon's and Kumok's eyes followed them, and Bongnyeo still didn't say anything, with her face buried between her knees. After all the men had jumped down, a swarm of girls followed behind, being dragged. They seemed to be about Soonboon's age.

"Girls!" Soonboon yelled in a low tone in spite of herself.

"Could they have been taken as well? Am I right?" This time, Kumok asked with chattering teeth. Instead of answering her, Soonboon watched what they were doing. Some of the girls had absent expressions, and some looked like they were about to burst into tears any second. Some didn't show any feelings whatsoever, and some girls were fidgeting, sneakily reading the officer's face.

The military policeman separated the men from the girls: "Now, you guys stand over there, and girls come here!" His voice resonated throughout the police station, waking up the gray night. People moved slowly, following his voice and pointed finger. He got closer to them, his face looked sinister. He began to kick some of the men. They recoiled.

"What stupid sluggish bitches you are! What are you guys going to do with such rotten mental conditions?"

The military policeman's hands, mouth and legs never rested for a moment. Meanwhile, a young police officer stood in front of the men with a big bundle from the warehouse. He suddenly dropped onto the floor as if throwing it away.

"Change into these clothes, and be thankful to the Japanese Emperor for providing you new clothes. From now on, you will live as proud Japanese subjects. If you don't obey, if you resist or run away, you will lose your life. Do you follow me?"

After he spoke, the police officer started to untie the bundle. When unfastened, clothes fell, stacked on top of each other. Tawny-colored uniforms with identical shapes, they seemed to all have been made in the same factory. There were only shell-shaped hats and working clothes.

"Form a single-file line and take the clothes one by one."

They took the clothes, changing out of their old ones and into the working clothes, following orders.

"Oh, my, how shameful," Kumok turned her head away, and Soonboon closed her eyes. They had seen men working without shirts on under the hot sun in the fields, but they had never seen men naked like this. After they had all changed into the same clothes, it was hard to tell who was who.

"Are you guys done? Then follow me. Don't even think about running away. You shall die if you are caught running away." After the military policeman threatened them, a sword on his waist, he took them to the grain warehouse.

Just then, someone began shouting among the men.

"Send a message to my family to tell them I'm fine and I will be back home soon."

The military policeman approached the voice angrily.

"Which son of a bitch said that? Who was it?"

"My family will be worried about me. Please tell them I'm here and that I'm all right."

The military policeman stopped in front of the man. All of the men's eyes were focused on him and the policeman. The military man looked him up and down, his eyes full of malice.

"Say that again. What did you say?"

"Tell my family…"

But his words were cut off in the middle by the policeman. Military boots flew up and kicked the young man right in the shin. *Ouch!* He dropped down on the floor, his knees bent. *Aah!* The policeman's boots kicked again, this time on his thigh. The man cowered on the ground. His screams became louder and sharper.

"Say that again."

"No, no, sir," the man answered, suppressing a groan.

"Did you guys see that? The same will happen to you if you ask any unnecessary questions. No questions are allowed, got it?"

The military policeman looked around at the men triumphantly. Their eyes were filled with fear and abandonment. Then he gestured with his chin, allowing the police officer to take them, smiling slightly at all of their horrified expressions.

"Okay, now follow me." Following his order, the police officer went ahead, and the men trailed behind without saying anything.

"Those sons of bitches!" Kumok said after seeing this happen, her teeth clenched.

Another policeman came toward Soonboon, the other girls behind him. The girls were afraid, their shoulders hunched forward. There were seven of them.

"They might have been abducted too." At Kumok's words, Bongnyeo opened her eyes and looked at them. Soon after, the door was flung open, and the other girls came into the room. Through the opened door, the chilly spring air rushed in, and Kumok shivered with the night wind.

8. Police Station

The commotion in the yard subsided, the darkness thickening and settling down heavily on the ground. This was not the same darkness that Soonboon had seen at home, it was not the same moon that held the starlight. When the whole world went dark, the police station was no longer hectic. Only bleakness remained. Sometimes, a deep sigh rushed into her ear, shaking the stillness. Deep moaning sounds wrung her heart, and fear kept her from sleeping. Both her fear and the cold made her extremely tired. Kumok came closer to Soonboon, folding her arms around Soonboon's. "I am cold." Soonboon was cold, too. Thin cotton *jeogori* and a skirt were not enough to withstand the chilliness of the spring night.

"I want to go home."

Soonboon grabbed Kumok's hands quietly when she spoke. She could feel Kumok's soft, warm arm under her breast.

"My parents are looking for me, aren't they?" Kumok said, talking to herself.

"Stop talking and get some sleep. Otherwise, tomorrow might be tough," Bongnyeo said in a small voice.

Soonboon could feel some power in her small voice. Kumok leaned her head on Soonboon's shoulder after Bongnyeo spoke. Her body now rested under Soonboon's chin. She had different smell and warmth from Soonboon's mom's. For now, Kumok and Bongnyeo were like her mom and her sister- a family she would have to depend on.

"I can't sleep. What will happen tomorrow?" Kumok started to talk again, after staying silent for a while. She was worried about what would happen the next day.

"Get some sleep," Soonboon told her with a lower voice.

"I can't."

"Try to sleep, though."

"I did, but I couldn't. The harder I try to sleep, the more I think of my mom." Her voice was soaked in sadness.

"Just close your eyes, or tomorrow will be harder," Bongnyeo said in a subdued tone, her voice rough, though she seemed to be asleep. She must have woken up while they thought she had fallen asleep.

"I miss my mom," Kumok said again.

"Get some sleep," Bongnyeo responded bluntly.

Kumok shut her mouth and sniffled, and Soonboon gently caressed Kumok's arms, looking at her as she whimpered. The girls tossed, turned, and sniffled, uncomfortable sleeping on a cold floor away from home. Beyond the small window near the ceiling, the pitch-black darkness sat like thick mud.

Cough! Cough! One girl started coughing. She had a slight cough since she arrived at the police station. She was short with a pale face and looked as though she was often ill. Her coughs stirred the darkness.

Soonboon fell into a short slumber without noticing it, her whole body immobile. In the middle of her sleep, she heard sounds. She was not sure whether it was real or a dream, or maybe the sound of wind. It was weak and intermittent. *What is that?* She was too drunk with sleep to recognize it. The sound continued and got louder and clearer. Someone was crying. *What happened? Who is crying? Is it my mom? Why is she crying? I should wake up and comfort her.*

Soonboon could barely push open her eyelids. Through squinting eyes, the world looked blurry and dim, as if covered with fabric or fog. It looked different than usual. *Where am I?* Strange objects filled the room and nothing was recognizable. Girls were crouched, hugging their arms around them, and only a small lamp hung down from the ceiling. When Soonboon saw the tiny window near the roof, she finally remembered where she was. She recalled what happened the day before and recognized the scene in front of her. *Right. I was taken while chasing the butterfly.*

Soonboon was startled awake suddenly; she figured out clearly now the identity of the sound hovering on the rim of her ears. A girl was crying, and trying to mute her voice. As if it were contagious, more girls started whimpering two by two. Crying was the only thing they could do now, and it had spread to all the girls in the room like a plague.

Then it happened. The iron door banged open, and the light turned on. Soonboon felt the bright light in her retina like a sharp pin. The girls were terrified and drenched in fear.

"What are these stupid bitches doing? You won't sleep well if I talk nicely. So I won't be nice anymore." A chief of police glared at them. The girls buried their faces, swallowing the rest of their tears to avoid his unflinching eyesight. One girl suddenly stood up, or rather she was forced to. The police chief had grabbed her by her braid. He yanked her head back and forth.

"It hurts!" the girl screamed. Her sudden cry at midnight rattled the air. The girls hugged each other, shocked by the screaming, watching the situation with half-awake eyes. The girl's eyes were shaking with fear. Her eyes resembled a cow's.

"It hurts. Please, let me go. Please…" But the police chief kept pulling her hair, and began to drag her away from the other girls. As she struggled, her shoes fell off, her white socks dragging on the bare floor.

The girl resisted, but the chief pushed her roughly, sick and tired of her strength. "This bitch!" His power was too strong, and he threw the girl up against the wall. Then something sparkled under the flashing light… It was a sword. The officer took the sword out from its sheath and struck the girl without any hesitation. The rest of the girls screamed, then shut their eyes tightly, instinctively. Momentarily, there was stillness again.

The sound of the chief officer's military steps walking away broke the silence. After it was over, the girls opened their eyes and pushed their bottoms backward, their eyes filled with fear. The girl's *jeogori* string was cut, and blood was gushing out between the strings. A red spot spread gradually, widely around her. Her *jeogori* was getting wet with blood, and sticking to her flesh. Her mouth was half opened, and she was sitting down on the floor as if she were going out of her mind. The blood gushed out, but it looked like the girl didn't feel any pain. The other girls' faces were pale. They couldn't have spoken even if they wanted to.

"Now you understand my meaning."

The chief looked around at the terrified girls with a nasty, satisfied smile. The girls turned their heads and looked down, avoiding his eyes. Soonboon wished she could vanish to somewhere else. *Poof!* She wished to either disappear into the ground or fly up into the sky. As long as it was a place where the police chief couldn't find her.

Finally, the chief pointed at another girl.

"You!"

His eyes were as sharp as a long nail, looking at her. The girls' eyes followed his finger. "You!"

Soonboon was terrified. *Is he pointing at me? Is the end of his finger pointing at me?* The finger was surely pointing toward Soonboon.

"I mean you, you!"

Soonboon's heart was pounding. No, she felt like her heart was beating so fast it would burst. Her bladder squeezed as if to urinate, and she felt excruciating pain. *Me? Not me...* She looked around at the other girls to make sure he was actually looking at her. Kumok hid behind Soonboon.

"You, come out here." His finger pointed at Kumok, not Soonboon. Soonboon shrugged her shoulders and twisted her body.

"Do you think you can hide from me? You little rascal!"

He walked with long steps, approaching Soonboon and Kumok with glaring eyes. Kumok was still behind Soonboon, trying to crawl away from the police chief, but there was no place to hide in such a small space. Before long, the chief began to drag Kumok away. She struggled with her one free arm.

"Let me go, please let me go!" she resisted strongly. Her arms could have ripped. But she couldn't defeat his power. After Kumok was taken, the remaining girls sat expressionless, blank. Their feelings were unutterably complicated; they felt relief for not being chosen, and also the fear of someday being called. They felt guilty, too, for not helping Kumok. All of these feelings were mixed up inside of them, singeing their mouths shut.

Just then, they heard an ear-splitting scream from beyond the wall.

"Don't do that, please don't do that to me. Please... *Ahhh!*" It was Kumok, begging and crying beyond the gray cement wall. Nobody could help her now, nobody.

Soonboon covered her ears with her hands. She heard something thumping against the cement wall. The screaming continued. Soonboon pressed her ears harder, but the sound squeezed in between the gaps in her fingers. It felt like the screams were chopping her body on the inside. *Ahhh, ahhh!*

Maybe it's a dream; maybe it's just a crazy dream, a nightmare, Soonboon repeated to herself. If she woke up from this dream, mom's smile and the sunshine and a peaceful morning would be waiting for her. Familiar daily life would come back to her when she woke up as if nothing happened. *Of course, it will. But how I can escape from this horrific dream? Please, I am begging, please, someone help me to get out of this dream. Let me wake up from this dream.*

Meanwhile, the day broke, but nothing had changed. The nightmare continued. Soonboon had never hated the sun as she did now, shining mercilessly through that small window. The girl with the wound on her breast had not slept because of the pain last night. Other girls had cut pieces of their skirt and tied them around the wound, trying to stop the blood from coming out, but bleeding had not stopped. Soonboon saw a person's gaping flesh for the first time. The hole in her skin was prominent, but Soonboon and the other girls couldn't do anything for her. The words 'cheer up' were meaningless. What the girl needed right now was medication and proper treatment. The iron door opened, and a policeman came in. His face looked as if he had a fitful night's sleep, his dry mouth was stuck with spittle.

"Come out now. Hurry up."

Soonboon stood up from her spot, and the other girls followed, all staring at the policeman's face. They hadn't stood up in a while as they had stayed shrunk up all night on the cement floor. Though they were still young, sleeping on the cold floor had hindered their ability to move.

"Little slowpoke bitches, why don't you move faster? We have a long way to go."

The girl with the chest wound stood up with the help of the other girls. Fortunately, the bleeding had now stopped, and was dry and stuck to her *jeogori*, stiff like starch. Her blood-soaked *jeogori* rubbed against her wound, making the girl groan, her forehead distorting with pain. Bongnyeo helped her by holding her hands and they followed the other girls out. The police officer sent them each out with a yell followed by a kick. Sometimes the kick came first. Soonboon and the other girls moved quickly to avoid his kicking.

This morning was different from any other morning Soonboon had seen. The sun was still bright but horrible. Soonboon realized that darkness was not the only thing that can trigger dread. She perceived at that moment that the bright, shining morning could be awful as well. The truck was waiting for them outside. It was the same truck that the police took last night to move the captured men elsewhere. On second thought, Soonboon had heard a noise when twilight shone through the small window. They might have been transferred at that point. She thought it had been a dream, but clearly it wasn't.

"Hurry, hurry up, it's a long way to go. We don't have time to hesitate," He rushed the girls in angrily. Soonboon climbed onto the truck bed, following the others. There she was in the truck, Kumok, who had been dragged out by the police chief last night. Soonboon was glad to see her, and pushed aside some other girls to get near her.

"Are you okay?" Soonboon asked, her face both glad and worried, but Kumok didn't answer. She just nodded her head, looking exhausted, empty.

Soonboon sat by Kumok, and Bongnyeo sat next to the wounded girl. *Roar! Roar!* Soon the truck started to move. The girls didn't know where they were going and what fate would be waiting for them. The truck rode onward, passing by dozens of villages, far away. As everything passed by them, Soonboon sobbed unwittingly, tears dousing her cheeks and covering them, so she held her breath.

Suddenly, she saw a white fluttering object. It was the butterfly that had led her to a beautiful spring field that day. But the other girls didn't see the butterfly's white, translucent wings. Only Soonboon could see them. The butterfly circled Soonboon, scattering white powder around her. Soonboon watched it with eyes swollen from tears.

9. Transit Train

A long, snake-liked train was waiting for the girls. Soonboon was wondering how its big heavy wheels would roll, but the worn down wheels seemed to slip on the rails immediately. There was no sign of the train's destination, and nobody had told them where they were going. The train looked like a centipede.

"This is your train. No chatting or disturbances allowed. Move along in perfect order."

But the girls didn't get on the train, they just stared at its long body.

"Don't just look at it, get on the train. How many times do I have to tell you, stupid bitches?"

The soldier forced the girls in with his wildcat eyes. The girls jumped down from the truck bed and climbed onto the train. Their movements were like white magnolia petals being torn from a tree, like pink cherry flower petals swept away by a dim gray wind. Bongnyeo, holding the wounded girl's hands tightly so she wouldn't lose her, came down from the truck and got onto the train. The girl wrinkled her forehead, feeling acute pain with every movement. Soonboon had never been on a train when she was growing up, this was her first time even seeing one. They had already ridden in the truck for a long time, how much longer would they have to ride the train? If they took this train, they would be farther apart from their parents, and it would be so much harder to get back to their hometowns.

Soonboon looked back over and over again in spite of herself. Her neck kept turning back, as if pulled magnetically. Then she noticed Kumok's un-natural steps.

Mihee Eun

"Did you get hurt?" Soonboon asked her, holding her hands, but she didn't answer. Something terrible must have happened last night. Looking closely, Soonboon noticed that Kumok had bruises on her legs and wrists. Soonboon guessed at what happened, but didn't ask. She thought it would be better not to ask.

"How about her? Is she going to be okay?" Soonboon asked Bongnyeo, worried about the wounded girl. Bongnyeo didn't say anything, and the injured girl bit her lip, trying to withstand the pain.

"All aboard?" The soldier counted the girls. After confirming that they were all there, he slammed the door shut.

"I miss Kiok," Kumok muttered to herself as the train started moving. She missed Kiok, not her mom, not her dad. Before Soonboon could ask who Kiok was, she continued talking: "My little sister, Kiok. Her eyes must be peeled looking for me. I should be taking care of her while mom and dad go to the field to work. She liked me even more than mom, but who will take care of her now?" Kumok spoke solemnly, her elbows resting on her knees, her chin lying in her hands. Her sorrowful eyes were far away, focused on nothing.

The train ran and ran, the vibrations spreading from the girls' buttocks to their spines. Soonboon had no idea where they were going, she couldn't even guess. They were neither in coach nor did they have any chairs. They were being imprisoned in the cargo. The cargo was confined, the sunshine cutting in like logs through thin cracks in the walls. They approached the cracks to see the scenery outside. It was both familiar and unfamiliar to them. The train passed by a valley, then broad fields the next moment, and then a river.

The girls were given a rice ball with pickled radish once a day. The cold rice balls felt like sand rather than being sticky, but the girls had to eat it since they didn't know when their next meal would be. Some girls urinated in the cargo, and others vomited. It smelled of musty urine, but they couldn't care. They were not allowed to complain or grumble. In the beginning, the girls grimaced, but now they were starting to get used to it. They realized it was not the time to scowl at or look down on their situation. These thirteen to sixteen-year-old girls were not human beings anymore, they were animals: animals that resembled humans. They were like cattle that would soon be sold at the market and displayed at the grocery store, they were not living people, and they were no longer their families' daughters.

Rattle! Rattle! The train gradually started to slow down its regular rattling rhythm. The girls' bodies could sense these small changes because fear and tension had sharpened their nerves. The engine hissed, the brakes squeaked, and then the train made a long, tired *choo choo* sound. The girls let out deep sighs that accompanied the train's sounds. Maybe the soldiers would let them out of the train now and they would call out the girls who wanted to urinate, allow them to do in a line, exposing their white bottoms to unwanted gazes since the girls not knowing when they would get another chance to pee.

"Come out if you want to urinate. Hurry, hurry, if you are sluggish you will be beaten."

The soldier's order was short and intimidating. The girls stood up slowly, taking the time to stand up since their bodies had been bent for so long. *Moan! Moan!* There was moaning here and there. Although the crying had stopped, it could start up again anytime. If one person started, all the girls would take it as a signal to cry again, and it would continue like bees swarming out of a hive. But no one wept now, though they wanted to. Their tears were on the inside. They bit their lips because the soldiers' whips and swords were glowering over their heads ready to strike them at any time. One girl's tears would only bring more desperation.

Soonboon stood up from her spot.

"I'm coming with you," Kumok said, following Soonboon. After jumping out of the confined cargo, they met the sharp wind in a field. Though the sun shined, the wind was fierce. It was not warm at all. Soonboon breathed in the wind, her eyes half opened. Kumok shivered from the chill, and her face turned a deathly blue.

"Don't go far. The train will start again soon."

Following the soldier's order, the girls looked around to find a proper place to pee. The soldiers kept an eye on them to watch for any runaways. The girls urinated, their white buttocks uncovered. Normally they would be shy about exposing themselves, because this body part was considered holy to them, but they couldn't be shy now. They didn't have any other choice in order not to pee on their clothes. Before they were finished, the soldiers forced them to rush back inside the train. All of a sudden, a sharp whistling sound rung in their eardrums. The sound was more shrill than usual.

"Stop there!"

A scream replaced the sound of the whistle. Everybody was surprised at the sound and turned towards it. One girl was running away from the train. The grassland lead up to a hill and three soldiers were chasing her.

"Get in, go inside right now!"

The soldiers cornered the girls as they watched her escape. They were pushed back toward the train, but they kept watching the girl as she ran. *Fast, fast, faster, run.* The girls stamped their feet impatiently, wishing for her to get away, but before long she was caught. The soldier who captured her wasted no time trying to talk to her. There were lots of girls who could replace this girl, they didn't need her. He took out his sword and took a swing at the girl's back. The sword cut through the air and then through the girl. The girl's scream split open the air. At the same time, another soldier lashed his sword at the girl indiscriminately, as the girls screamed and watched the scene in horror.

The girl, struck, looked as though she was trying to turn around, but she fell flat on her face, blood gushing out from her stained white clothes. It was a dark crimson red. Her blood, redder than a camellia and sweetbrier flower, kept gushing out. Her body was now immobile. She was dead, and nobody cared. A naïve teenage girl, once a precious daughter of a family, was dead and left deserted in a field. Her body would now become the prey of wild animals, or rot and soak into the earth. Or maybe it would turn to fertilizer for the grass and trees, or her soul would fly back to her hometown.

The other girls' faces turned deathly pale. They knew now that death would always be hovering around them. A sword could take their lives at any moment. It all depended on the soldiers' caprice whether death would reveal itself and take another girl's life with it. Knowing this made their hairs stand on end.

"See, any fugitive will be dead like that, so if anyone else wants, run away."

The soldier who had killed her threatened the other girls with poisonous eyes. The girls knew that his threat was no lie. The cruel, dirty sword that had killed the girl was ready to strike once more at any moment, just like that.

The girls didn't cry, for some reason they couldn't. Perhaps it was their fear of death, or that their minds had gone blank.

"Go back inside." The girls climbed back onto the cargo neck and neck, chased by a whip. The soldier lashed his whip continuously. *Whip, whip*, the girls heard the whip cut through the air in all directions as they climbed back into the dark and smelly cargo.

The train started to move again without any pause to consider that a girl had just died. A flower-like youth, the age that filled with lots of dreams; the girl met the death at this age without any reason. Only the reason that she was born at a weak country as a daughter of a colonial land. The girls were not allowed a chance to feel sorrow or to cry for her death. The evidence of her death would be forgotten soon, but her existence was deeply soaked into the girls' consciousness. They could be dead as the girl at any moment; she could be their future.

Rattle! Rattle! The train moved on into the unknown world, never resting. The poor, scared girls crouched in the train's cargo, not knowing what awaited them at their destination. Soonboon shut her eyes. Maybe if she shut them she would be able to dream the dream that she wanted to. She might meet the butterfly again or perhaps her mom and dad. But what came to her mind was only the face of the dead girl.

"Will we make it home alive?" the girl next to Soonboon asked, her quiet voice coming from between her knees. Her voice cracked, not having spoken for so long. Soonboon couldn't answer her question. She wanted to ask the same question herself.

"How were you taken?" she asked Soonboon again.

"I was out in the fields chasing a butterfly. How about you?"

"I was going out to get medication for my father."

"Wasn't there anyone else? Were you the only one who could go out for the medicine?"

"I have two brothers, but my eldest brother was forced to join the army, and the other was hiding to avoid the draft. I had no choice."

She raised her head and looked far away. She had a round white face, the wing of her nose broad and elegant. Another girl interrupted their conversation.

"I was taken while weaving a straw bag. I was at home as usual when they came into my house all of a sudden and took me."

"I followed them, trusting that they would let me pursue my studies."

Other girls began chiming in.

"Will we actually work at a factory?"

"Or will we be nurses who take care of wounded soldiers?"

The girls spoke, worried about their uncertain futures. But nobody could tell for sure where they were going or what they would do.

10. Busan Harbor

After many hours had passed, the rattling sound of the train slowed. The jerking stopped and the train came to a halt as it finally reached the station. The girls looked at each other, wondering where they had arrived. The train had brought them to Busan Harbor located at the southernmost part of Korea, and they were forced again to jump out of the train. Getting off the train, Soonboon faced the ocean for the first time in her life. She had never been to Busan, never taken a train or spent the night at a police station. All of this had happened after leaving her home for the first time.

Soonboon had lived under the shade of her parents where her bones could grow stronger as a young girl. The low back mountain in front of her house blocked the wind on windy days, and the sun always shined peacefully on her house. The fields and narrow valleys held the sun in their pockets, the stream ran slowly across the field, the branches of a willow tree stood by the creek. Legends were everywhere, and stories helped the town children grow strong and well-behaved.

Soonboon had grown up listening to these legends. A pond where a virgin drowned had taught Soonboon carefulness. A scope owl that sang in front of the mountain predicted that year's harvest. The sad story of a housewife who jumped down from a cliff three or four times taller than her gave a lesson her to have good manners as a wife. Those stories had been told from generation to generation and they were landmarks for her as she matured.

She always knew that she would leave her home someday, at the time of her marriage. She imagined leaving with rouge on her cheeks and forehead, wearing an elegant dress, ready to begin her new life. She never thought that she would leave her hometown like this. She kept wishing everything was a dream. *Surely it must be a dream.* Perhaps if she closed her eyes and opened them again, everything would be back to normal. But, but… though she closed her eyes and opened them again, everything was the same.

Busan was entirely different from her hometown. There were a lot of people there, the wind was humid, and the air smelled strange and salty. She realized later that this was the scent of the ocean. Her hometown smelled of sweet earth and the pungent smell of trees. But this smell of the salty sea and humid air mixed with cars and people made her dizzy. The strange scene triggered more of Soonboon's fear. Perhaps if she were visiting this place with her parents, she would have felt curious and excited. But now, by herself, Soonboon was only afraid. The girls were handed over to a new set of soldiers who were waiting for them, as if they were military supplies for sale.

"Move fast, lazy bitches! Look at how sluggish you are!"

The soldiers scolded them as usual. The Japanese passed by, sneaking peaks at the dozens of wandering girls. Some wrinkled their faces as if they were looking at stinky garbage. Soonboon followed the girls in front of her and looked back over and over again. *Will I make enough money to buy the land for dad?*

"I miss my mom," Kumok said to herself behind Soonboon. Her shoulders were down, and her steps were weak.

"Hang in there. They might beat you." Soonboon held Kumok's hands and kept pace with the other girls.

"Can we ever come back if we leave now?" Kumok seemed about to burst into tears. But Soonboon couldn't answer. Bongnyeo was walking slowly, helping the wounded girl. Her steps were still slow, and it was hard for her to walk straight. Her face still grimaced with pain every time she took a step.

"Bongnyeo looks like an adult," Kumok said, looking at Bongnyeo helping the wounded girl.

"Don't you know chatting is not allowed?" an approaching soldier told them with glaring eyes, catching them unaware. Kumok was afraid and walked faster to catch up with the other girls.

"Sluggish, stupid bitches. What good is that attitude? Huh?"

The soldiers were always peremptory. If they weren't yelling, they were shouting swear words at them. They could strike them down with their swords at any time. They had already stolen one girl's life, and another was wounded.

Her life was leaking through the crack in her flesh. Soonboon and the other girls were forced onto a big ship anchored at the harbor. Her eyes opened wide. Both Soonboon and Kumok stood tall, looking at the big ship. They couldn't believe it. How could such a massive iron ship float on the water without sinking?

"On board. Hurry up, there is no time to hesitate." The soldier glared at the girls as he forced them into the ship. *Honk! Honk!* The huge iron ship spurted steam as people climbed aboard the ship.

Just then, one of the girls resisted stubbornly, unwilling to go further. Two soldiers pushed her, grabbing her arms, but she dug her feet into the ground.

"I am not going. I want to go home. Please let me go."

Her begging shook the smelly harbor. She fought back with her legs, but was dragged. Her shoes and socks came off with force, her backside wiggling in resistance, but it was useless; she couldn't defeat their power. It was the girl who had been caught getting medication for her father. She struggled stubbornly to escape their hands. But as she struggled, her skirt was ripped, the string of her *jeogori* torn off. But they still didn't stop.

"Please let me go. Please, I don't need any money, just let me go home."

"This bitch doesn't listen when I talk nicely. Okay, fine, go if you want. I won't stop you, go."

One of the soldiers who had grabbed her seized her hair and dragged her to the quayside. The girl was screaming, and then disappeared. They had pushed her into the water. It had happened in a blink of an eye. Soonboon couldn't believe her eyes. Maybe what she saw was just an illusion, but no… it was real.

The girl floundered in the water. "Rescue me, save me." One girl ran to her and tried to save her, but she fell head first into the water. The soldier who had thrown the first girl in pushed the second girl in as she sought to help her. They needed to sacrifice some as an example to control the other girls. These two girls were the example and the sacrifice. If one person made trouble, more people would follow, so they cut the sprout of the resistance where it grew as an example for all.

"Did you all see that? If you want to go home, tell me anytime. I will let you go back."

The remaining girls cast down their eyes, looking down at their feet. They couldn't look the soldiers in the eyes. Soonboon looked at Bongnyeo worriedly. She bit her lips, her face stiff. Her expression was dangerous as if she might make trouble herself.

The girls went on board one by one, followed by Soonboon. When she stepped on board, she had a weird feeling that was different from walking on land. She felt like the land moved away from her instead of staying firm like the earth. Her body wobbled. Soonboon felt depressed thinking that this jiggling and shaking might be her future.

Another group of girls was already at the cargo of the huge ship. Where did all these girls come from? Their faces were not so different from the faces of Soonboon's group. They must have also been caught and brought here. Death was not uncommon; it was everywhere around them. They could be killed in an instant. To die was easier than to live here, and this was their future.

Bongnyeo helped the wounded girl sit down and sat by her. The blood had stopped gushing out, but the sword wound was open and infected. The swollen wound was oozing pus; it was so gross to look at. She was sweating and her forehead knitted in pain. Soonboon approached her. If only she had a clean fabric, she could clean out her wound, but there was no clean material anywhere.

"Is she going to be okay?" Soonboon asked, looking at Bongnyeo's face and at the wound interchangeably, but Bongnyeo didn't answer. This made Soonboon even more worried.

"Let me see."

Soonboon got closer to the girl, walking on her knees, and opened her *jeogori* to look at the wound. It was more serious than she thought. The wound was filled with yellow pus, running down on the sides. Soonboon brought her mouth near the wound and started to suck the pus out before Bongnyeo could stop her. Her mouth was filled with sticky liquid, she unwittingly knitted her forehead while holding foul-smelling pus in her mouth. Soonboon looked around for a place to spit out the nasty pus as she held it in her mouth.

"Oh my gosh. How dare they hurt a person like this? They probably take better care of their animals at home. Sons of bitches!"

"It's okay. You don't need to do that," the wounded girl stopped Soonboon who was sweating as she sucked more pus out.

"Is there any clean fabric? I need to wipe it out," Soonboon asked, looking at Bongnyeo and Kumok. Blood began gushing out again from the wound. Needless to say, there was no clean fabric anywhere. The girls' clothes were dirty after not having changed in a few days, and they didn't see any other material with which to clean the wound. Bongnyeo remained quiet. She knew that she couldn't do anything for her. Comforting her verbally was not actually helpful for the wounded girl. Bongnyeo shut her mouth, incapacitated. The injured girl knew that something was wrong, and looked down at her wound with fear.

"Thank you," the girl said. Her voice was weak.

Soonboon sat by her and fixed her posture, so she was leaning on her shoulder.

"What is your dream? Mine is not unusual. I want to have a good marriage like my mom and my sister. Isn't that funny? How about you? What do you want to be?" Soonboon asked while rubbing the back of the girl's hand. Tears were rolling down her cheeks.

"I want to be a singer. Like Nanyoung Lee. But now…" she said, full of tears, for she had more tears than words. Soonboon wanted to listen to her sing. But she couldn't ask her to sing since she was in so much pain.

Honk! Honk! Just then, the sound of the boat horn went off, signaling their departure. They must be leaving the harbor now. The girls burst into tears they had been holding in their hearts. Sniffling sounds were heard here and there. They would never go back to their homes, never see their parents or sisters again. As the horn sounded, Soonboon's eyes got wet with the tears that she had kept reserved for so long. *Honk, honk…* Her nose burned with sorrow.

I'd better say that I can't go any farther. Should I jump down from here? If I die here, my soul will go back to my hometown, and I might be less alone and less afraid. If I'm lucky, maybe I will survive.

Choo! It honked again, followed by a mournful echo which spread far away. Then, a girl stood up and approached the door, but was blocked by the soldiers. She was about to be thrown amongst the other girls but swung her arms, resisting stubbornly.

"Please let me down, I want to go home."

The girls' wet eyes all stared at her. Their eyes seemed to have already lost their fighting spirit. A couple of girls had firmer gazes as they anticipated their unknown futures, but sometimes their courage changed back to fear. Nobody on the ship knew what their futures held. The soldier with a glittering insignia preached, looking around at them.

"You were drafted to the war as citizens of the Great Japan. Remember your country, and be loyal to the Great Japan. If your country doesn't exist, you don't exist, either. The country has the first priority, the second is the country, and the third is the country. Take action after asking what you can do for your country. Be honorable so that you can have the chance to be loyal to your country."

Soonboon didn't understand. *What the hell does he mean by honorable?* Japan was not her country. Her home was the small village of Suncheon, Jeolla Province. Her duty was to behave modestly, get married and make a family. She didn't have any greater ambitions than that. She wanted to live like her mom, her sister and the other women in her village and wished to leave this world after that. Why were country and honor so important now?

Soonboon realized that something was going terribly wrong.

• • •

11. Death of the Girl

The girls spent a numb night in the cargo, and met the sun in the morning. The fearful morning had turned to afternoon, and become a blackish night. Then it turned to the morning again without fail. They had a meal once a day: a rice ball mixed with salt. They ate it so they wouldn't die, they slept so they could live, and gave up their dreaming so they were able to survive. The girls with seasickness vomited and drank no water, but they couldn't leave the cargo. They only had two options if they wanted to leave: either tolerate it until they arrived at their destination or die in the cargo.

Sometimes they wanted to accept their destiny, but other times they felt its unfairness. Packed in the cargo like luggage, their faces turned pale from the stale air. They couldn't urinate or sip water freely. They were not permitted to move of their own volition, though it was impossible to escape in the middle of the ocean.

Soonboon was curious about what was outside the cargo. She just wished she could see the boundless ocean and cobalt sky. She wished to see the horizon, the sparkling water, and the clouds being propelled by the sea breeze. Though she wished to see all these things, she couldn't escape the cargo.

From now on, her body was no longer hers, her life and her dreams were no longer hers. The future was not hers, and time was not hers, either. She was the Japanese soldiers' property and accessory, one that could be disposed of at any time. Rights and sanctity were bothersome theories for the soldiers. The girls were not human beings, and they should not request to be treated as such.

Soonboon sensed that the wounded girl leaning on her shoulder was not normal. Her state was worsening, and her body temperature was rising, but it was not because of the uncirculated air inside the cargo. The girl was sweating profusely, her lips drying and turning white. Her wound gave off a smell of death. Soonboon touched her forehead. Her temperature was hotter than she had expected.

"Get up, wake up."

The girl looked at Soonboon with slightly opened eyes, then closed them again.

"Something is wrong."

Soonboon looked at Bongnyeo worriedly, but Bongnyeo was calm as if she already knew what would happen. Soonboon realized that the girl might die if she didn't do anything for her right now.

"I can't stay like this. Take this girl for a minute."

Soonboon got up, handing the girl over to Kumok.

"Where are you going?" she asked Soonboon, putting the girl's head on her arm.

"I am going to ask for some medication."

"Don't go." Kumok stopped Soonboon worriedly.

"Am I supposed to just watch her like this?"

"You might get in trouble, though."

"It'll be okay. Wait. I'll be right back."

"Don't go," the girl barely grabbed Soonboon's skirt as she lay in Kumok's arms.

"Don't go. It's useless." Her face strained to talk.

"Hang in there a little bit more. I will bring medication."

"It doesn't matter."

The girl barely shook her head. Her eyes neither contained worry and fear of tomorrow nor the desire to live. They were empty, as if she had abandoned her life.

"I am sorry, I'm just worried about Soonboon," Kumok told the girl, excusing herself as she smoothed down her hair. She must have felt sorry that she almost stopped Soonboon from going. After Kumok had spoken, the girl's eyes moved from Soonboon to Kumok. Her weak eyes said, *I know, I understand.*

"Wait, I will be right back," Soonboon said sternly.

"Don't go." Kumok stopped Soonboon again, but Soonboon pushed the other girls aside and approached the entrance.

"Please give me some medication. A girl is dying, give her some medicine."

Soonboon banged on the door of the cargo, *rat-rat-rat*. All the girls' eyes moved toward her. She hit harder, *rat-rat-rat*. Someone heard it, turned a key in the lock and opened the door.

"What happened? Why are you making this noise?" A soldier looked angrily up and down at Soonboon.

"Give me some medication. A girl is dying," Soonboon begged, rubbing her palms.

"Where is she?" the soldier looked around at the girls.

The girls turned away or looked down to avoid his eyes. Soonboon pointed at one girl to lead his eyes in the right direction.

"There she is," Soonboon indicated with her finger.

He went forward, following Soonboon's finger. The girls scooted aside to make room. With each step forward, new space was made and he stepped toward to the girl, Soonboon behind him. As he reached the wounded girl, her body slumped on the floor. The eyes that had looked at Soonboon just a few minutes ago were now staring at one spot. Soonboon approached her to wake her up.

"Open your eyes. Hang on."

But her body was shaking at Soonboon's fingertips. Blood and pus from her wound had stained her *jeogori* yellow and she seemed to have no power left. Her barely opened eyes were not closed this time as if she was unable to close them. She must have known she couldn't open her eyes again once they closed. Someone sniffled next to her, and the sniffles radiated outward like a spiral.

"Be quiet!" the soldier yelled, his fierce eyes looking at the girl who didn't wake up no matter how much Soonboon shook her. The girls swallowed their sobs and wiped away their tears, fearing the soldier.

"Pull her out." The soldier ordered Soonboon with his chin. She tried to carry the girl on her back, but the body was heavy and kept slipping, and Soonboon's knees were bending under the weight. Finally, Kumok helped her carry the girl on her back. Bongnyeo was looking off into space. Soonboon approached the entrance, holding the girl on her back. Suddenly she felt warmth on her back, and shallow breathing. *The girl is still alive, she is still breathing.* Soonboon was sure that the girl was still alive, breathing weakly. She felt sorry for this poor breathing. The other girls moved aside again to make space. Soonboon walked in the empty spaces and exited the cargo.

She felt the hot and humid air outside. It was much better than that of the confined cargo. Only the smell of fish filled her lungs as she took deep breaths. The sun reflected on the water. Without knowing what would happen, Soonboon was dazzled by its reflection. Tens of thousands of schools of fish twinkled. Or maybe these are the scales of the ocean. If the sea were alive, the schools of fish would be its scales. Or were they butterflies? Being outside after having been imprisoned for so many days, Soonboon's eyes could hardly handle such bright light.

"Drop her."

Soonboon let the girl fall on the deck, following his order. The girl slid down as if almost dead. Just then Soonboon saw them lift her from the floor and drop her into the blue ocean. The ocean swallowed her, rippling white waves in a second showing it had taken her, then calmly reflecting the sunshine again.

"This is all for you. She would have died anyways. If you left her like that, the infection would have affected all of you," he told Soonboon as she stood there in shock at what had happened.

All of a sudden, his burning eyes began searching Soonboon up and down, and he approached her slowly with lustful eyes. Soonboon stepped back: one step, another, and then one more. When she couldn't move back any farther, blocked by the wall, he stepped forward. The brim of his hat almost touched her forehead. Soonboon couldn't breathe; his sunbaked pore-filled face and thick mustache moved as he spoke.

"You look delicious. *Yoi*. Good."

Soonboon didn't understand. The Japanese government forbade them from using Korean, making them speak Japanese instead. But it was hard to throw away their mother tongue, and even more difficult for Koreans to learn Japanese.

"She is valuable." He raised Soonboon's chin up with his index finger. His finger felt like a wooden stick, and she could feel his strength. She breathed in his sticky smelling sweat. She didn't even think of turning her head aside to escape his touch. She looked down to avoid his eyes that flew at her like a knife. After seeing the wounded girl tossed to sea, Soonboon had no desire left to resist him. His hot, humid breath fell on Soonboon and made her curse. He ordered to his subordinate standing beside him: "Take her inside."

When he finally removed his finger, and gave the order, Soonboon almost fell down on the deck. The subordinate dragged her, inserting his arm through hers. She was dragged and taken back into the room, but it was not the same room where the other girls stayed. She was placed in a small room located on the opposite side of the cargo. After pushing her in, he stood blocking the entrance. There was a small bed against the wall and a small desk next to the bed. All the furniture was tied firmly on the floor to keep it from moving with the motion of the waves.

Soonboon had a feeling in her gut. *Why did they take me here, why didn't they take me back to the same room with the other girls?* She was worried about the soldier's beady eyes and realized that the only way to escape from this room was to die as the wounded girl had. *Shall I die? How? How can I die?*

As Soonboon was lost in thought, the room's owner entered with a wicked smile. When he entered the room, the soldier blocking the door saluted, then left the room. The officer began to take off his pants. He was in a rush and his hands slipped as he tried to untie his belt. Soonboon shrugged her body and moved into the corner.

"Come here. You resemble my sister- my little sister in my hometown."

After a couple of failed attempts, his naked lower body was finally revealed. He approached Soonboon in the corner, walking on his knees. She couldn't bear to see his undressed body, having never seen a man's naked body with its dangling penis between the legs.

"If you listen to me, you will survive. If you don't, you will die in this room. Those are your only options."

Huuh! A burning smell came out of his mouth. The strange burning stink of his hot, humid breath gave her goosebumps. He dragged her to the middle of the room, holding her legs hard. Soonboon struggled against him, but her resistance was useless at this point. He dragged her down like an inanimate doll.

"No, please don't do that. Please, please…"

Soonboon moved back, pushing the floor with her legs. Her backside hit the floor painfully, and he grabbed her skirt. His strong arms easily ripped it off and he positioned himself on top of her body. Soonboon tried to push him away, but he was strong like a mountain. Just then she felt a hard object enter her body. She tried to escape, rolling and twisting her legs over and over again, but his strength was hideous and undefeatable. At last she gave up all resistance, and his member, deep in her body, began fluctuating inside of her. Soonboon felt a horrible pain as if her organs were coming apart, but he didn't care about her suffering. *"Argh! Ahh!"* she groaned as her genitals started bleeding, as he moved his pelvis back and forth even harder, smiling awfully, satisfied with seeing her blood.

The world shook with his movements and her dreams for her future broke desperately into pieces. She closed her eyes to escape the man's panting above her, wishing her body was deep down in the ocean. Just then, she saw the butterfly floating to her. *Butterfly, butterfly, where have you been? Where have you been, butterfly?* The white butterfly fluttered softly inside her eyelids.

12. Future, Disappeared

The girls' eyes focused on Soonboon when she came back to the cargo. How did it go? Where had she gone? Soonboon shed tears as they looked at her. They all realized and understood what had happened though she said nothing. They were aware that it would happen to them someday too. Their face darkened as they let out a deep sigh for their fates, which were likely to be the same as that of the disappeared girl.

"Where is the girl? What happened to her?" Kumok asked in a little voice when Soonboon came back to her spot.

"…I sent her off."

"Sent her?"

"…I just…sent her off."

"Then, what did they do to her?" Kumok asked obstinately.

"Why are you so curious about it?" Bongnyeo asked Kumok abruptly. Bongnyeo's sudden scolding silenced Kumok, and she put her chin in her hands on her knees.

"The girl might have gone anywhere, so don't worry about her. She might feel more comfortable where she is now than she would be here," Soonboon said, staring in one place.

"Comfortable? She will be the prey of the fish in the ocean," Bongnyeo cut Soonboon off again gruffly. Soonboon shut her mouth at Bongnyeo's harsh words.

It is not bad to be a prey of the fish. If I became a prey of the fish, I could swim, at least, and go wherever I wanted. It would better than staying here like this. Far,

far away, swimming in the ocean, getting caught by a fisherman's net someday and put on my parents' dining table would not be so bad. Then I could be the flesh, eyes and thoughts of my parents, live as a part of them. If I could live like that, I would never apart from them, I would not be afraid anymore, and I would be comfortable again. Soonboon imagined that this would be better than her current situation, but she didn't say so out loud.

After the wounded girl had died, no more girls said anything if they were sick. Even if someone else was sick, they didn't mention it to the soldiers. They just endured, suffered, and hid. Although their bug bites oozed, and pus ran and rotted, they withstood and overcame.

Every day was tough because of the seasickness which Soonboon felt as well. The moving floor felt like loose earth instead of firm ground, and made them vomit. They could hardly even eat the salty rice ball provided them once a day. If they vomited, they were whipped, and if they resisted, military boots flew to kick them. There was no mercy with the cruel whips and boots. The girls had lost their self-esteem thanks to the cruelty of being stepped on, smashed, and kicked. They pushed aside all their memories of who they were, whose daughters they used to be, and who they wished to be in the future. The soldier who had raped Soonboon searched the girls every night. He took Kumok, other girls who obeyed quietly, or else he took Soonboon again. Every time the girls were called and came back, they avoided eye contact with everyone. Soonboon knew the reason they all stayed silent.

How many days and nights passed, and how many times did the sun rise before the ship finally stopped? As the deafening engine sound went off, a strange silence rushed into their ears. The girls instinctively walked on their knees toward the crack, looking out through it. The ship had anchored at harbor. The cargo was now full of turmoil. Loud, busy sounds came from beyond. The trembling sounds of an iron ship resounded like an echo, moving through their bodies in tiny vibrations. But the engine sound still hovered in their ears like an audible hallucination.

"Where are we now?" they wondered, looking at each other. Footsteps outside of the cargo sounded different than usual. The girls' instincts told them that they had finally made it to their destination. They had stopped by several places along the way, and the girls diminished in number at each unknown location. The ship had stopped by an island for a while when a wind storm had come, and girls were gradually taken out to a harbor. Six girls in one place, ten in another, sometimes they were dropped off in even bigger numbers. The empty spaces in the ship grew as more and more girls left. Fortunately, Kumok and Bongnyeo had not been separated from Soonboon. Kumok was still worried about the outcome of the journey, her innocent eyes always struggling to find an answer, but Bongnyeo kept her mouth closed and spent her days angry.

"Where are we now?" Kumok looked around.

"Are we in Japan?"

"Not sure."

"It's too hot."

Kumok's flushed face was sweating. Soonboon thought it might because of the heat from the engine, but it was not. The air was sticky and humid, making it difficult to breathe. Sweat escaped from pores all over their bodies even though they weren't moving; it was even hotter than summers had been in their hometowns.

"I heard the weather in Japan is more humid than in Korea. We might be in Japan."

"No, it is not Japan, it is much farther. We came far, far away, there is no way we can find our way back home now," Bongnyeo mumbled to herself. It was the first time she had spoken in a long while. Much farther? Kumok frowned and began to sob at these words.

Whether they were in Japan or not, it didn't matter. They were far from home, and far apart from their parents. They didn't know where they had arrived, how far they had come. They had no idea in which direction they had come either. Even if they were allowed, they didn't know how they would get back home. How could they go back home without money, without a safe place to sleep, without being able to prepare food? They must only follow the soldiers' orders now. And even if they were obedient, they might not survive. Kumok's shoulders shook more and more, her eyes flooding with tears.

13. New Job

Click! Finally, the locked door opened, and an intense sun from an unknown land frightened the girls who had been in the darkness so long. Soonboon felt like the clicking sound of the cargo door was the sound of the world opening. The girls held each other's hands instinctively, without anyone forcing them.

"We should not be separated, never, ever. We are all one family here, we should live together or die together."

"We are one, no matter what happens." Fathomless fears soaked the teenage girls' eyes.

A camouflage-uniformed soldier stood at the entrance with an annoyed face. He was short, so the sword on his waist was almost touching the floor. The sun on his back revealed his body like a silhouette, and he said to the girls with a high-pitched voice, "Pay attention. This is where you will stay from now on, so get off. Get out of here and don't leave anyone behind. Don't be sluggish." He banged the wall of the cargo with his stick, hurrying the girls out threateningly. The girls followed his orders, leaving the cargo filled with fear and curiosity over what would happen next. They squinted their eyes under the bright sunlight. The heat was scorching. The soldier handed them over to another soldier along with a name list in his hand. After receiving them and the list, the new soldier began calling their names one by one while checking their faces.

"Get on the truck. Hurry, hurry up. Don't be lazy!"

This soldier was even more impatient than the previous one on the ship. He shouted and cursed right away without any reason. Soonboon and others got on the truck, chased by his curses and his stick. Their faces burned in the hot air and their bodies were showered with sweat. The humidity and sticky air made them tired quickly. For once, at least, it was not cold: a bright spot in their misfortunes.

The truck drove on and on along the bumpy road, spurting loudly and emitting clouds of dust. Whenever the truck shook on the rough road, Soonboon and the others felt burning pain in their bottoms. The truck ran without stopping and without caring about the girls' pain. Carsickness returned to them and Kumok covered her drooling mouth. She had not eaten anything for days because of seasickness, so only saliva came out from her mouth.

"I feel like dying," Kumok said, patting her chest with her fist. Her eyes were weak from sickness, hot weather, and dust clouds. Soonboon patted Kumok's back lightly with her fist.

"It must be hard for you, isn't it?"

Kumok nodded her head instead of saying yes.

"Where are we going now?" Soonboon asked as if talking to herself when she patted Kumok's back, but nobody could answer her. All the girls were looking at the passing scenery, emotionless. The landscape was unfamiliar to them, the houses were different from those in their hometowns, and people's face looked different from theirs. This unfamiliar scene made them yearn for home even more. *What are mom and dad doing now? Maybe they are working with bent backs in the field as usual.*

"Are we going to make money?" Kumok asked Soonboon with a half doubting voice. "Do you remember? The officer said that we could make money if we listened to them well," Kumok kept asking Soonboon, swallowing nausea-induced saliva.

"Money? What money? They are not the type of people to pay us. I heard a rumor that they prey on girls," Bongnyeo answered before Soonboon said something.

"No way. They are not devils, murderers, or vampires, so how would they prey on us?"

"Bad news travels fast," Bongnyeo answered in a mutter.

A devil, a murderer, a vampire… The harsh, foul words stuck to Soonboon's neck. No way, they must have families of their own: a sister, or a mom. If they are human beings, they won't do things worse than a beast, but… they were not people. They were too cruel and merciless, so what more could they expect from them?

None of the girls knew what to expect. They hadn't realized that a fate was opening its mouth, waiting for them to fall in and never allow them to escape. In that moment, they had not yet figured this out; rather they were not able to imagine what would happen to them.

The weather was unbearably hot. They were stifled by the heat even if they did nothing. Their unwashed bodies emitted a nasty odor, and were sticky with smelly sweat when touched. They itched everywhere because of the sweat; rather, their current lives were one big itch.

How far had the truck gone? Houses were seen only sparsely. Soonboon's eyes caught site of a long house among them. It looked like a temporary barrack rather than a house, barbed wire wrapping all around it, big guard posts standing on both sides, and soldiers walking around inside holding guns. The barbed wire looked cold and evil, and Soonboon's recent experiences told her that this was where they would stay. Just as she thought, the truck drove straight toward the barrack.

The sun was setting down slowly, and dusk was settling in. It was always the same at this time of day: the flying birds would return to their nests after throwing the wind away on their feathers. It was a mystery how they found their nests again after having flown so far away. They flew back precisely to their yards again and again. When the sun started to fade, the world was covered with gold, birds returning to their nests holding the twilight on their backs. Soonboon used to feel some sorrow at this time of day. Distant sadness raised its head from deep inside her heart, and it dug deeply.

Soonboon's eyes stared far away and remembered the familiar scene at her home around this time of day. Mom came back home as the birds flew back to their nests, and she made a fire in the furnace. The soft crackling of the fire sounded like birdsong, the smell of burning firewood filled her nose, and white smoke seeped out from the furnace. Though their table was not abundant with food, mom felt happy as she prepared dinner for the family. At this time, mom's efforts were satisfied and the food was ready; it was always exactly at this same time of day.

Soonboon realized that another day had passed. Time passed, days ended, and angry blood circulated inside her body in this cruel circumstance. She missed everything so much she almost teared up: the birds, her mom, the smell of burning firewood, the sound of her parents mumbling to each other…

"Can't you move any faster?" the soldier rushed the girls along. Each time he spoke, his eyes gleamed, wielding his commander's stick threateningly. The girls got off, holding tightly the bundles that dust had accumulated on. Soonboon got off as well. Her hips were numb with pain after hours of riding on the bumpy, rocky road. When they went in the direction they were forced, two guards stood on both sides. It was a spine-chilling sight. Two more soldiers came from the barrack, and stood in front of the girls.

"This is where you will stay from now on. Each person will have one room, go and find the place that has your name on it."

One room for each individual?

"The only thing you need to do now is to be absolutely obedient. If you listen to me well, you will survive, if not, you will die."

As one soldier spoke to them, the other with a sword on his waist walked around Soonboon and the others, thoroughly looking them up and down. When he saw Soonboon, he smiled slightly as if he was satisfied with her. His smile made her hair stand on end.

"You should throw away everything from your past: your habits, the thoughts that you had yesterday, including your families. In here, your family is the soldiers of the Japanese Emperor, so focus on comforting them with your heart. To serve them means to serve the Great Japanese Emperor. Therefore, do not behave carelessly. The ones who resist will not be forgiven- they will have only death. Put the bundles you brought down on the floor."

The girls looked at each other and dropped their parcels obediently. The old packages were taken, and new clothes were distributed to them. It was a Japanese pajama, *nemaki*, opened in the front.

"This is the cloth you must wear from now on. Change into these clothes when service time comes. These are the rules: get up at 7 in the morning, wash and clean the room. If necessary, clean or repair the soldiers' uniforms. You should eat your breakfast by 9, if you are late, you can't eat. Your next duty is to comfort the Imperial Japanese Army. If you don't obey, you shall die. There are more rules you should follow. First, you are not allowed to play together. Second, no chatting. Third, don't get close to any one particular soldier. Fourth, never say anything outside about what you see here. Just pretend you didn't see it, even if you saw it, act like you didn't hear anything even if you heard it. Finally, never, ever run away. If you get caught, cruel punishments await you. You will survive if follow these rules, if not you will die."

Death, death stayed close to them no matter where they went, this one thing was for sure. Death, which is met only once in life, loomed over them. This was not the only place where death was common, no, it was common in their hometowns as well. They would hear of someone's death here and there, a wailing cry fluttering in the wind like floral leaves. They had heard lots of stories about people being tortured and sliced to death with Japanese soldiers' swords. But now, death was in front of their noses. Girls were beaten and threatened, the sword was able to strike at any moment. Soon, death became nothing to them.

14. Room 3

Musty damp smells overwhelmed Soonboon as she entered the room assigned to her. The room allocated to her was Room 3, Kumok was in Room 2, and Bongnyeo in Chamber 4. How fortunate it was to be next to them. A wooden floor was connected to the wall, *tatami* was spread out, and two blankets were strewn on the wooden floor. There was nothing else. The room's plainness, the *tatami*, and bleak unfamiliar features filled Soonboon with pungent fear and sorrow. Girls in other rooms craned their necks to look at Soonboon and the other new arrivals. Everyone seemed to be about Soonboon's age, fifteen. One girl waved her hand toward Soonboon, her round face and short height telling Soonboon she might be Korean. She looked different from the others with their flat low-bridged noses and brown faces.

Ring-ring, rang the bell, and the girl's face disappeared. It was already dark out, the zodiacal light vanished and objects revealed their borders in the darkness. Suddenly, Soonboon saw the same Korean girl standing next to her room.

"You are extremely unlucky. How did you come here?" she said, looking at Soonboon pitifully. The girl wore a single *nemaki* and walked around Soonboon as if she were her own sister.

"Are you Korean? Where did you come from? How old are you?" she asked very curiously without waiting for Soonboon to answer.

"I am from Suncheon, and I'm fifteen years old."

"Suncheon? I am from Sangju, Kyungsang Province. It must be spring there, and the forsythia and azalea must be blooming already. The azalea on my back mountain had exceptionally beautiful colors," she was tracing her memories, staring into the distance.

"By the way, what are we going to do here?" Soonboon had been very apprehensive about what she would do there. The girl snapped out of her memories slowly and stared at Soonboon.

"Do you really have no idea what you will do here?"

Soonboon nodded as she asked. The girl looked at Soonboon for a while and finally answered glumly. "Just do whatever they tell you. Don't think about doing anything else, then you will survive."

She didn't answer her question about what particular work they would be doing. All she said was, "You will figure it out soon." Then she went on to say that she was eighteen years old, and had been caught while she was washing clothes at the well.

"There are lots of girls like me here. Most of us came from Korea. Two Japanese women live here, but they stay in another place. Be careful of them, they mainly serve the Japanese officers. They are mean, so be very aware."

Ding, ding. The bell clang again.

"It's time for meal distribution, let's go. Don't look around, don't try to know anything. And no speaking Korean allowed, no singing Korean songs, either. If you don't follow these rules, you will be beaten. You have to be very careful since they are even crueler than you can imagine..." The girl walked ahead, leaving Soonboon's room.

Soonboon tried to follow her, but stopped and turned back to Kumok's room. She drew back the curtain and entered the room. Kumok sat in the middle of the *tatami*, her emotions clearly melancholy.

"Let's go. They are distributing our meals."

Kumok turned her head and looked at Soonboon.

"You need to eat. If you are hungry, you will be even more sad. So let's go, eat and cheer up." Kumok stood up slowly from her spot on the floor, convinced by her words. Soonboon went to Bongnyeo's next. She was sitting on the floor holding her knees, refusing to open her mouth.

"We are going to eat, come with us. Don't think too much about everything, let's just go and have a meal. We can think after we eat."

Bongnyeo didn't answer.

"Let's go."

She still remained quiet, feeling no pressure from Soonboon.

"Stand up. Come with us. After meal time is over, you won't be able get any food, so stand up." Now, Kumok was trying to persuade her. Kumok tugged on Bongnyeo's sleeve, making her stand reluctantly.

The girls looked around nervously, holding their meals from the meal distribution station cautiously. But Soonboon lost her appetite when she received it; she had no desire to eat, perhaps because of her exhaustion or carsickness.

"Eat. If you don't, you will lose your appetite more, so eat even though you don't want to right now to gain your appetite back," Kumok said, looking at Soonboon worriedly.

"Eat it, if you don't want to die. You can survive if you eat," the girl that had visited Soonboon's room said, agreeing with Kumok, then added, "That woman is the one from Japan."

She whispered, pointing at a woman wearing a *kimono*, then bit into her rice ball as if she hadn't said anything. After the Japanese woman had walked across the comfort station, she went into the military station with some officers.

Soonboon and Kumok went to Bongnyeo's room and saw that she was just fiddling with her rice ball. Just then, heavy sounds of hitting and swearing came from the other room. *Smash, smash*. Whenever the dark sound repeated, someone cried and begged.

"Sumimasen, sumimasen."

Soonboon turned her head toward the sound. A girl fell down on the floor, a soldier smashing down on her with his boots. It sounded like he tripped over her and fell down. Soonboon couldn't stand this moment. But, if she intervened, she and the girls might not be safe, either. Her experience so far had taught her this much: pretending she had seen nothing would be better for the girl in the end. In the meantime, after fiddling with her rice ball, Bongnyeo finally brought it into her mouth. The rough way she forced it into her own mouth meant she was not hungry, but angry about something.

"Go back to your room when you're done."

The soldier forced the girls along, and they stood up hurriedly, gulping the remains of their rice balls and water.

15. Meeting the Butterfly Again

Soonboon teared up staying in her small room by herself. *Where am I? How far away from home am I?* She could only think of these questions, and was afraid of how much she didn't know. Fortunately, sounds from Bongnyeo's and Kumok's rooms helped to relieve her fear. *Knock, knock.* Soonboon knocked on the veneer wall. *Knock, knock,* Kumok answered. *Knock, knock:* she knocked on Bongnyeo's wall this time. *Knock, knock,* Bongnyeo responded as well.

Soonboon opened a small bag the soldier had given her a while ago and took out a small soft object that looked like long dried peppers. She was curious about what it could be, having never seen this kind of object. It was a condom, shaped like a small rubber balloon. But Soonboon had no idea what it was or what it was for. As she turned it over, looking at it on all sides, the curtain lifted, and someone entered her room. It was a Japanese officer with a sword on his waist and a yellow label on his shoulder.

"Hmmm…It's a new girl. *Yoi.* Pretty! Good. Your name is Haruko from now on. Haruko, how do you like that?" Repeating the word *yoi,* he started to take off his pants. His hands hurried as if he was in a rush to urinate. After taking off his shirt and pants, he approached her, naked. The penis between his legs shook hideously. Soonboon moved back in surprise.

"Oh, my gosh, what are you doing? Move back." She retreated, her bottom scooting along the floor as her arms swung.

"You will survive only if you listen to me. Otherwise you shall die. Obey me absolutely."

He approached and pulled off her clothes, the noise of her clothes ripping resounding, her naked body exposed. She resisted, sticking her crossed arms into her arm pads, but he only moved his pulsating member closer toward her. She struggled under his legs, but couldn't fight the young man's strength. She kicked him with all her might. His face turned from pale to red as he rubbed the spot she had hit him.

"Bitch! How dare you insult an officer of the Imperial Japanese Empire as a *Chosenjin?*"

Soonboon moved back at his hurtful words, but there was no more space to move back. He took out his sword.

"You deserve to die since you don't know how to comfort an officer of the Imperial Japanese Empire. Do you want to listen to me or not? Decide. If you don't obey to me, I will take your liver and eat it."

Soonboon stared at him. Her face was full of fear. All of a sudden, she heard the sound of the sword dividing the air and felt the sword strike her body. Everything happened in the blink of an eye. Soonboon shut her eyes very tight, then everything stopped — no sounds, no lights or movements. Perhaps this was the feeling of dying. She felt pain on her shoulder a while later. When she opened her eyes, bloody flesh gaped open on her shoulder, blood gushing out from the wound.

Soonboon's strong resistance would soon slip away through the opening in her flesh. The soldier smiled wickedly at the blood and at her surprised face, then pushed her down, inserting his erection into her body. Soonboon twisted her legs in defiance.

"You bitch! Are you still out of your mind? Do you really want to die?"

He widened his eyes with anger and seized her neck, stifling Soonboon's breathing. She scratched the back of his hand, struggling and wriggling. At the time of her almost death from suffocation, he loosened his grip on her neck and kicked her thigh instead. His merciless kicking forced her lower body to uncoil. The pain felt like it would rip her whole body, starting with her legs. This was a different pain from the wound in her shoulder.

Bongnyeo's scream was heard from the next room. Soonboon heard shrieks coming from the other rooms as well: from Kumok's, from the other girls' rooms- the screams erupted all around. The rough veneer walls shook, *thump, thump*. "Please save me. Please help me. Please don't do that, please…" Soonboon fainted, hearing Bongnyeo's screaming from the next room.

How much time had passed? When she woke up, another soldier was on top of her. He was panting, inserting his penis into her body, his face full of sweat. She wanted to push him away, but her hands were tied up and lifted over her head. Soonboon bit his chin, and he slapped her face until it turned to the side. His ignorant roughness caused her nose to bleed.

"Are you crazy enough to die?" his eyes glared murderously. He might have killed many people on the battlefield and this place might be the same to him. To kill or be killed: he was still alive after having killed the enemies who tried to kill him, so killing someone was not difficult for him at all. Soonboon fainted again.

When she woke up, her hands were still tied up. She couldn't guess how many hours had passed, or how long she was unconscious. Fortunately, the bleeding from her shoulder had stopped. Now she could understand what the girl had said: *'If you obey them, you will not die.'* Another soldier entered her room as she woke. He shouted upon seeing her bloody shoulder.

"Kitanai, kitanai."

He was no different from the former soldiers, though he called her dirty. As the others had done, he untied his belt, took out his genitals and raped her. She didn't know how many soldiers had come. One, two, three, four… The counting was meaningless. Soonboon wished her body would wear out and turn to dust. If she was worn down to the size of an ant, she could sneak away. Then, nobody could see her, and nobody could violate her. The soldier was moving his waist roughly on top of her as the others had. Soonboon didn't have any power to shout, and no tears were left to cry.

She closed her eyes so she wouldn't see the soldier's greasy face. At that moment, she missed her butterfly. She yearned for the white butterfly that floated over her head in the spring field. She wished to have wings and fly away from this place. She shut her eyes tighter as his panting got louder. Just then, a white object fluttered inside of her closed eyes. It was the butterfly. *Flutter, flutter, flutter… Butterfly, please take me somewhere else, please…*

Long lines of soldiers formed in front of the girls' rooms that night, as usual, each of them waiting for their turn to rape the girls. Girls' screams leaked out here and there from under the doors.

The night grew deeper and deeper.

16. A Haircut

Everything had changed. The girls were no longer living as they had once before. The girls had more days left than they had already lived, but their lives seemed segmented, ruined. The morning sunshine glared into Soonboon's room through the curtains, and she heard busy sounds from outside. One never knows what will happen in life, but Soonboon knew her present was pitiful and her future will be miserable.

Soonboon felt like she was in a casket. She inhaled and exhaled, lying in the long narrow room. If her breathing stopped, would the pain disappear? Although she was alive, it was as if she were dead. She heard Bongnyeo sobbing in the next room. Soonboon was relieved to hear that she was alive because she had heard Bongnyeo's cries to a soldier to save herself throughout the whole night.

Then, the curtain opened, and Kumok crawled to her.

"You are alive!"

Tears pricked her eyes when she saw Kumok squirming towards her. She lay down next to Soonboon and held her hands. Her soft hands shook slightly.

"Good job, well done," Soonboon said to comfort her, but she herself didn't understand quite what she meant- whether it meant she had endured last night well or that she had made it out alive. Kumok didn't say anything, and Soonboon had nothing to say, either. They just lay down holding each other's hands in silence, but the silence contained more meaning than spoken words. Soonboon understood well how Kumok felt about it although they didn't say anything about last night. Because of this, Soonboon was sorry for her.

"How is Bongnyeo doing?" Soonboon lifted the curtain and looked outside. The girls stood in a long line at the hand basin and restrooms located at the end of the hall. Soonboon moved toward Bongnyeo's room, Kumok following her like a shadow. Bongnyeo, who had screamed and moaned all night, was crying as her genitals were bleeding. Kumok began to cry as well. The tears that they had kept inside flowed down at Bongnyeo's cue.

"Don't cry," Kumok consoled Bongnyeo.

"If we die here, it will be the most meaningless death, so let's tolerate it. We need to survive," Soonboon said, not understanding why she said this at this moment. She felt a strange feeling about Bongnyeo. Her sobs and dark face made it look like she had decided to die soon. Although Soonboon had spoken against death, she didn't know if it was better to tolerate a meaningless life or to put an end to it. It might be better to die than to withstand this humiliation. But, but...

Soonboon missed her mom and dad. Though her life with them was impoverished and needy, it was joyful. She missed her dad's quiet laugh and her mom's warm touch. When winter came, mom made a fire in the furnace for the family. When Soonboon lay on her stomach on the heated floor, looking at the fluttering snow, she felt an unknown yearning. She didn't understand what it was. But this yearning continued to bubble inside her until she stepped down into the snow-filled yard. Outside, she made a chrysanthemum by stepping in the untouched snow, tracing her steps in a circle. She missed the snow mingling with the cold. She also missed the azaleas and forsythia that bloomed in the spring. Now that she thought of it, they looked like a dream. *Will I live to see them again?*

The morning sunshine coming into her room through the curtains was already high in the sky. But it was a different morning than any she had seen so far. It felt shameful, humiliating, cruel. Now, she understood why her friends in the village hid so carefully, hurrying to get married to avoid virgin delivery. They had understood its true meaning.

"What are you doing here? Move. Fast. Did you forget the rule? You should not get close to anyone or talk to each other," a woman lifted the curtain and came into her room.

It was a Japanese woman who supervised the comfort station. She looked around at Soonboon, Kumok, and Bongnyeo all together and spoke with a stinging voice, showing the whites of her eyes.

"You've already heard the rules: you should not leave your room so thoughtlessly. You know that you will get punished if you break the law. Fine,

I will forgive you since it is the first time and you don't know this place well. Now, go wash and clean the room and finish your meal."

She was talking in Japanese, her slanted eyes constantly moving. Timid Kumok went to her room, pushed by the woman's scolding. Soonboon was worried about Bongnyeo, but knew nothing would change if she stayed with her, so she went back to her room as well.

"Wash and have breakfast, then you will get a haircut today. The women of Great Japan have bobbed hair. You should also have the same hairstyle. You will get punished if you don't obey the order. After that, I will provide medication. You should take one right now, and the other should be used to wash your private parts after you are done servicing the soldiers. Your entrance shouldn't be dirty when you are serving the soldiers, so always be aware of keeping your private parts clean."

A soldier talked with a loud voice, pacing back and forth in the hall. His high-pitched voice echoed loudly. He continued. "You should appreciate the Great Japanese Emperor for letting you eat and sleep without starving. You must be thankful for his grace, you dirty *Chosenjin*."

The soldier lifted the curtain of Soonboon's room and yelled, "What is this lazy bitch doing here? Didn't you listen to what I said just now?" Soonboon arranged the dirty room and blankets, and rushed outside. Whenever she moved, she felt pain in her shoulder from last night. The girls were lining up to the meal distribution station to receive their rice balls, and Soonboon stood at the end of the line.

These firmly lumped rice balls with pickled radish were the only food they were provided to eat. Sunshine settled down on the riceball, reflecting shining pieces, and flies gathered at the smell of rice. Numerous black flies sat on the riceball and crawled onto the back of her hand. Following the rice, they moved onto her lips, and gathered on the blood clot on her shoulder. Soonboon tried to shoo them away, but they wouldn't leave. They flew all around her, lured by the smell of blood and rice. Soonboon carefully swallowed a grain of rice. Her mouth was so dry, the rice scratched her tongue like sand. She tasted nothing. She alternated between taking one bite of rice and drinking a sip of water. Tasteless humidity melted inside the water bowl.

At that moment, she saw a handcart coming toward the comfort station. Soonboon almost dropped her bowl in surprise. A pale leg slipped out on one side of the cart, which was covered with a straw bag. A small foot with a black sole. Whose foot was it? Soonboon's hair straightened on end at this moment,

77

and she quickly ran into the comfort station. She lifted the curtain and looked in Bongnyeo's room: she was not there. Only dark shadows lurked there. Soonboon's heart started to beat. *Boom, boom, badum, boom, boom, badum.* She felt like her blood was running backward in her veins.

"Bongnyeo! Bongnyeo!" Soonboon called Bongnyeo in a small voice, but she heard no response. Soonboon's heart kept pounding. No way, no way… Soonboon looked around the meal distribution station again. The girls snuck a peek at the dead body in the handcart, covered with straw bags under the bright morning sunlight. Sorrow and wrath filled their faces. The unknown girl in the handcart was exiting the last scene of her life, seen off by the other girls. It was a rest that could only be provided by death. Someone was sniffling. It sounded like a requiem for their incapability, for their powerless country, for irrevocable time and the for dead girl with the little soles.

"You should not die."

Soonboon heard a sound, but she didn't know what it was, feeling dizzy as the sun glazed over the dead body.

"Soonboon, don't die. Don't be an idiot."

Soonboon finally turned around. Bongnyeo mumbled quietly next to her, looking at the dead girl.

"I won't. You also should not die," Soonboon cried, tears reddening her eyes.

They ate without wanting to, they lived without wanting to. Soonboon ate for Bongnyeo, stuffing the food into her mouth although she couldn't chew or digest. Food stuck in her solar plexus each time, but she forced it down to her stomach with water. She decided to eat for Bongnyeo and Kumok, though she didn't want to eat at all.

"Whoever's done eating, come here for your haircut," a soldier shouted from the front yard of the comfort station. His eyes could not be seen under the brim of his hat.

"Do not be slow. Form a line quickly. I will count to three. If you don't make a line by the time I'm done counting to three, you will all get punished. One, two, three!" His piercing voice shook the fresh morning air.

One, two, the girls followed each other into a line. Some soldiers were searching the rooms to drag out the girls who refused to get a haircut. A scream came from one room, and the sounds of beating and pulling came from another. Soonboon poked her head out toward the sound. It was one of the girls from their ship. She struggled intensely, resisting the soldier who tried to pull her out, but as a young girl, she couldn't overpower him. She was dragged out to the front yard like a cow being taken out to be killed. She bawled, clutching the unruly soldier's hand as it grabbed her by her braided hair.

"I will repeat myself once more. There exists only death for those who disobey orders," the soldier shouted through clenched teeth. The girls obeyed hesitantly, glaring at the ground as his voice pressed upon them.

"If your hair is braided, let it down. After your haircut, go to your room and comfort the Imperial Japanese Army gladly."

The Japanese lady, who had been waiting with scissors, approached the group of girls and started cutting their hair. Dull scissors cut through their dark, unwashed hair. Saying no to this was not an option. Soldiers were standing in front of them with threatening faces, holding swords and guns, and the Japanese lady held out the scissors to the girls ominously. The girls left their hair to her helplessly. They shrank away as the scissors touched their necks, but the scissors cut swiftly. *Snip, snip*, went the terrible sound of cutting. They breathed in and out carefully with the feeling that the scissors might dig into their throats if they moved an inch.

Once a girl's hair was cut, someone's quiet sniffling could be heard under the sound of the scissors, but the sniffling didn't last long. It was cut out just as the hairs had been with more curses, and threats.

These were the hairs their mothers had combed and braided with love. These were the hairs their mothers had washed with boiled iris water on *Dano*[4] in May. Moms braided their daughters' hair, inserting red silky strings at the ends on New Year's Day. As the scissors passed by their hair, the girls felt emptiness and sorrow. *Snip, snip, snip...* How terrifying that a valuable part of them was missing now, how scary that something that should be treated with importance was now gone. They felt awkward touching the straight edges of their short hair. All the girls got an unnamed injection after getting their haircuts, and nobody told them what kind of injection it was.

Bongnyeo wasn't walking well.

"I think she's been beaten a lot," Kumok said, gesturing toward Bongnyeo with her chin.

"What about her wound?"

"I don't know, she didn't say anything else. She didn't even answer me."

Bongnyeo was that kind of girl who seldom talked about herself.

"By the way, who was the girl in the handcart a while ago?"

---

[4] **Dano** is one of the Korean traditional festivals that falls on the fifth day of the fifth month of the lunar **Korean calendar**.

"I don't know. Nobody said who she was," Kumok answered.

"You there, stop. What are you chatting about? Didn't you know you're not allowed to talk?"

A soldier who had been watching them approached and kicked Kumok's thigh.

Ouch! Kumok screamed and then quickly swallowed her words.

Soonboon made up her mind that she would live a new life to accompany her new hair and clothes, but it was not possible for her to change her past habits and feelings in one day. They had been soaked too deep inside her mind and heart to come out of her so easily.

17. Embittered Life

It was 9 o'clock in the morning. After confirming that all the girls got haircuts, the soldiers forced them back into their rooms.

"If you are all done, go back to your room and comfort the Imperial Japanese Army with all your hearts. Hurry up!"

Soonboon went back to her room along with Kumok and Bongnyeo. After that morning's turmoil, her mind and heart were muddled. As she began to breathe normally again, a soldier came into her room, lifting the curtain. She shouted in spite of herself. She would never get used to this job, even if she knew obeying orders meant survival.

"What are you doing?"

Soonboon moved back to escape from him. But he rushed into her with bleary, unfocused eyes. Screams and curses came from Bongnyeo and Kumok's rooms just like the night before. Soonboon closed her eyes, unable to do anything as the soldier's disgusting smell consumed her. He twisted Soonboon's hands and weakened her by kicking her thigh before putting his penis inside of her. Soonboon pushed him back with all her might. At that moment, a sharp pain flowed through her body like an electric shock. She didn't know where the pain had come from. As she struggled to push the soldier off, she got blood on his military uniform wherever she touched it. The blood that had circulated in her body now just gushed out, when her hand slammed down on his uniform.

She realized that he had stabbed her palm with his knife.

"You bitch. Are you never going to pull yourself together? Go to hell. How dare you put your dirty blood on me, bitch! You dampen my mood. What a buzzkill!" He beat Soonboon with his fist, feet, and the back of his sword. He smacked, struck, and trampled her body. She shook like dried straw under his fingertips. After she had fainted and was lying down, he finished his job on top of her. After he had left, another soldier came in right away. She heard the sounds of Kumok's painful breathing in the next room. She didn't want to see anything or hear any sound, either, so she closed her eyes tightly and blocked her ears with her hands. A white object flew into her closed eyes. *What is it? What is this?* She opened her eyes to look at the flying white object, but all she could see was the soldier's face as he rode on top of her. The man drooled sticky saliva and rubbed his red eyes as he panted on top of her body. She didn't know any of their names; they all went away after they had done the same cruel things to her. They were all wearing the same uniforms and hats. When she turned her eyes to the side to avoid his face, she saw another soldier who was watching her through the curtain. He hurried the naked panting soldier as if he was in a hurry to urinate.

"Come out quickly. Damn, I can't stand it anymore. Finish as soon as possible." He pulled out his penis and shook it like he couldn't stand to wait. *This is hell. Here is hell.* Soonboon shut her eyes again. The white object came into her eyelids again. *Flutter, flutter,* the object floated inside of her eyes. Butterfly, it was the butterfly: the butterfly that attracted her in her hometown and the butterfly that she lost in the field. It was gliding across the scenery of her closed eyes. Soonboon chased the butterfly in the darkness. *Butterfly, where are you going? Butterfly, don't go. Please take me wherever you go, please...*

After one soldier went out, another came in. Then another went out without saying goodbye, without worrying about her, treating her like a mannequin, like a fallen flower petal on the ground. And another came in. They rushed into her room and crammed their penises inside of her, ejaculating their semen on top of her body or inside of her body hurriedly, then left as the next pushed his way in. It seemed like something only animals would do. The fifteen-year-old girl's body that had been chaste and holy was being ripped and mangled over and over.

18. Comfort Station, Military Club, Game Room

All the girls who were taken by force had resisted fiercely. They had been found and abducted by Japanese soldiers without any reason while washing their clothes at the well, or doing work at home, or while walking along the road. The girls wished to deny and run away from the barbarism present in the barrack, so they cried, almost stopping their breath, but there was no way to escape the surveillance.

Time passed, days passed, and months passed just like that. Nothing was normal, yet the girls got used to their lives by giving them up. Abandoning hope and adapting to the reality saved their lives for now, but slowly drove them toward death.

"Everyone gather together. The Imperial Japanese Army will have training today so they won't come here. However, you should not play after eating your expensive meals. When the army is fighting as risking their lives, you should not do nothing. I will assign the work that you have to do, so gather up!"

A soldier with a gun on his shoulder called them, stomping around the hall with his boots and lifting their curtains. Soonboon went outside, but she felt pain in her lower body whenever she walked. All her organs were in pain as if they had been ripped apart by all the men's parts pushing inside her mercilessly. But then, how could her body feel ordinary after having intercourse with dozens of soldiers every day? Blood trickled down Kumok's leg as she walked, and Soonboon approached her. The distance between her and Kumok got smaller, and Soonboon whispered, watching the soldier's face.

"What happened to your leg?"

Something sliced through the air- it was a whip.

"No chatting allowed. Don't you bitches know that? How dare you speak in Korean here?"

He approached Soonboon grimly, and kicked her with his heavy military boot. She couldn't breathe, having been kicked right in her side. She walked faster now, caressing her wound. Kumok moved away from Soonboon, glaring at the soldier. Suddenly, a girl was dragged from the comfort station, half-dead. Two soldiers brought her out, their arms entwined with hers. She was slumped over, her bare feet dragging limply across the floor.

"Any bitch who hurts the Imperial Japanese Army deserves to be punished."

The whip unfolded on her small body. Once, twice, three times, her body curling up against the sticky strap. Each time the whip thrashed, her body bounced back.

"Your life is worthless. You are not a person, so obey my order absolutely. If you disobey, you will not survive."

The girl didn't move after that moment. There was no groan, no scream and no cry, her body drooping as if she were sleeping. The girls were stunned to silence as they looked on, but their fear spread like a disease, covering them like a blister. *Hiccup, hiccup*, Soonboon hiccupped. She stopped breathing to quiet her hiccups, but the air lingered inside her body and bubbled up, leaking out in a weird metallic sound. She blocked her mouth with her hands. The soldier who had lashed the girl with a whip began kicking her again. She was shaken powerfully from the force of his kicks and yet there were no signs of life in her.

"Check her out." The soldier holding the whip pointed with his chin to a soldier with a gun on his shoulder. He approached the girl and put his hand under her nose.

"She's dead. She's not breathing," the soldier told his superior without any emotion.

"*Bakayaro, bakayaro*. Idiot. Dump her out!" he ordered, spit flying through his teeth.

She was dragged out the same way she came. This girl who had breathed with them, shared eye contact with them, and felt homesick with them until now was dead. Soonboon didn't understand who was the idiot: if he meant the dead girl or the soldier who had killed her.

"Did you bitches see that? This is your destiny. No one is on your side. You only survive if we survive, so you should assist the army to join the battle without any worries, without any problems. If you hurt the soldiers, you will be killed like that dead bitch. Do you understand?"

The girls were at a loss for words, so they looked down to avoid eye contact, terrorized.

"Okay, now I will divide you into two groups. You will wash uniforms and sew them for two hours. Lazy bitches will be punished. Wash the clothes so they look like new and clean the buttons until they shine. Well-cleaned uniforms will encourage the army. Their confidence and self-esteem come from clean military uniforms, so work with all your hearts."

After these orders were given, two soldiers brought out two knitted bamboo baskets and put them down in front of the girls. They were filled with layers of dirty military uniforms.

"Repair these before you start to wash them. Hurry up!"

The girls acquiesced, forming two lines in front of the baskets. They searched the uniforms for any missing buttons or rips. The clothes smelled like gunpowder and death. Mud was stuck to them like fish scales, which shattered into powder as the girls flattened them out. Some uniforms were ripped along the elbows, some had lost buttons. Soonboon brushed off the dried mud, then she threaded a needle.

She remembered the night when she had helped her mom make a comforter for her sister. She threaded the needle so mom could decorate the quilt that her sister would use on the first night of her marriage. She had thought it would be the same for her. She believed that mom would make a beautiful, fluffy comforter for her wedding night, too. She used to dream about opening a new chapter and leading a new life as she opened her own comforter from her mom. She imagined that she would have her own babies, take care of them as they grew, and one day watch them get married. She could no longer wish for these things. Where did it all fall apart?

"I will run away. I will escape even though I might be killed. I will surely run away."

Soonboon couldn't believe her ears. She must have heard wrong. An old memory might have caused her to hallucinate.

"Are you going to stay here?" Bongnyeo whispered softly, looking around.

Soonboon stared at the military uniform and replied like a ventriloquist, "What? What do you mean? How are you going to get out of here? You don't even know where we are."

"It's okay as long as I'm not here. I just want to get out of here. I don't care where I go as long as it's not this place."

"We should find out where we are before going outside."

The wound on her shoulder was healing, and the wound on her palm was now just a scab. Time was medication, and time was poison too. Indeed, life goes on even despite horrific pain.

"I will go. I will surely go," Bongnyeo said, convincing herself.

Her tone was firm and determined. Soonboon wanted to run away, too. She wanted to get out of here rather than live here miserably. But how would they be able to escape this place?

As she sat, she felt pain in her swollen genital area. Soonboon recalled how the soldiers had dropped into her room consecutively, without even a pause. There were lots of weird soldiers, plenty of sons of bitches who requested strange things. Some imitated the mating of dogs and horses, some got an orgasm as they hit her. They were not like human beings, they were lecherous.

Soonboon squatted as if to urinate. Kumok and Bongnyeo crouched down beside her. They could understand each other's pain, though they didn't say it; it was sadder to say it out loud. It was abnormal to feel no pain, considering what they endured all day except for meal time. They were not allowed to have any breaks, they were not even given a chance to wash their genitals. If one person was slow, the next soldier rushed him out, ready to violate in turn. If someone fought back, she was punished by death. A girl called Kim, Duknyeo who had come here with Soonboon died after her nipples were bitten. Chunsim died as well, because her vagina was too small for penises to fit into, so they cut her pubic area wider, and her wound got infected. A girl called Ramiko was kicked so hard in her genitals by a Japanese soldier after she didn't obey his order that her uterus fell out. These stories transferred by word of mouth through the barrack instantaneously. It could be their turn anytime if they were unlucky. They must follow orders to survive, they must be deaf and blind.

"Finish quickly, you lazy bitches! These uniforms are for the Imperial Japanese Army, you better deal with caution," a soldier said in a high-pitched voice as he approached a girl and kicked her. His kick flung her aside. Soonboon grabbed Bongnyeo's hands as she tried to stand back up. They forced the girls again right after they finished washing the clothes and sewing them.

"Go back to your rooms. Hurry up."

Whistling resounded. The kicking came first. They kicked the girls first with their military boots and then started yelling. The whips in their hands were faster than their boots. The girls scrambled to their rooms to get away.

"Be tolerant. Hang in there whatever happens. You cannot succeed if you take reckless action, so be very careful," Soonboon whispered to Bongnyeo, holding her hands firmly before entering her room. Bongnyeo's expression said nothing.

The soldiers must have finished their training, because a soldier entered her room as soon as she got back. Short and with a sunbaked face, he rushed into Soonboon, breathing his bad breath directly in her face. She kicked him unconsciously, repulsed at the disgusting smell. He slapped her, her face twisting to the side from the force. He bound her hands and lifted her skirt. A dull sound came from Bongnyeo's room. The veneer wall shook heavily from the shock of something being hit. *No, no, Bongnyeo! Don't do that, please don't do it*, Soonboon mumbled. She felt all strength leave her body at the sounds coming from Bongnyeo's room. The firm, stiff penis was forced inside her and was already moving back and forth. She hated the feeling of someone's flesh inside her. Her lower body was in intense pain again. It was as if her uterus was being ripped apart. Soonboon shut her eyes and saw the butterfly floating behind her closed eyes again. The butterfly waved to her with its wings as if to follow it. *Let's go, let's go, butterfly. It is fine, as long as I'm not here.* Soonboon followed the butterfly.

After the soldier had gone out, another soldier came in. But he was different from the others. He was naive, and his military uniform was ragged. His eyes looked shrunken, and he didn't approach her with glaring eyes as the others had. He was quiet.

"Why don't you just do it? Do it quickly," Soonboon asked firmly as she lay down.

"Just lay down, I don't want to do it."

He was Korean, drafted into the Japanese military by compulsion. She was both glad and ashamed. She got up and adjusted her clothes.

"Where do you come from? I am from Suncheon," Soonboon asked him.

One of the rules here was that they should not have any close relationships with a particular soldier, so unnecessary chatter was not allowed. The girls were merely sex supplies for the troop, to be shared by all. They warned the soldiers not to get close with the girls. Warning signs were hung on the walls, telling them not even to be nice to them.

Comfort station, military club, game room: these were all names for the comfort station.

"Did you say Suncheon? I am from Yeosu, right near your hometown."

Soonboon liked him only because they came from the same place, but she knew she should not. She shouldn't like him. She was fed up with even hearing the word 'man.'

"By the way, can you tell me where I am? The trees are different, and the language is different from Japanese. Where are we?" Soonboon had been curious about it since she had arrived the comfort station. The man looked at Soonboon a while before responding, "It is Burma, far from Korea, farther than Japan."

Burma... She had never heard of it, she had never even heard about this country in a dream.

"By the way, how did you come here?"

"I came here in a compulsory military draft."

"We have the same destiny."

Soonboon was sorry for him, his fate and hers were almost the same. He didn't know how long he would survive, and she didn't know about her life, either.

"Please excuse me. I feel like I am going to die, please don't do it and just stay like this. Let me take a rest for a while."

Soonboon begged. Evidently, she felt like she was about to die. He sat there without saying anything as she begged, then he left the room. The spring breeze came into her room through the door as he left.

• • •

19. Dreams of Death

Soonboon crept out to the hallway as the bell rang to notify them it was time for dinner. She knew this was not a life fit for human beings. Men raped, abused and humiliated her like they were starving beasts. They didn't care whether or not she begged to die at their touch. If she turned her body aside with pain, they beat her, kicked her, and cursed at her. There was nowhere to run away, she couldn't defeat them no matter how much she resisted. If she didn't open her legs by herself, they did it for her. When they climbed on top of her and shook her, she swayed like a dried branch.

Soonboon took a deep breath. The humid, tropical air filled her lungs. Just then, Kumok came out from her room. She also crept out, unable to walk normally. Her face was contorted with pain. Only the girls could understand the burning pain, their young bodies covered in the filth of unsolicited sex. Soonboon looked toward Bongnyeo's room, she hadn't come out yet. Soonboon turned toward her room and peeked inside carefully, but it was quiet. *Knock, knock*, Soonboon called softly to Bongnyeo, but there was no answer. *Knock, knock*, she signaled again, but there was still no response. Soonboon returned to Kumok.

"What about Bongnyeo?"

"I don't know. She didn't answer even though I knocked twice."

"Is someone still there?"

"Maybe, but it was quiet. It seemed like nobody was there."

"Is she sleeping?"

Kumok looked at Bongnyeo's room worriedly as she caressed her lower abdomen. It would be okay if she were asleep. They should not interrupt her now.

"Let's go. We'll share our food with her." Kumok crept ahead, Soonboon followed.

Afternoon sunshine lengthened the shadows on the ground. Big leaves looked black under the sun, unseen birds calling out to their mates, *Chirp! Chirp!* It often rained here. It could start to rain in an instant. After the rain, a strong, pungent smell of trees and earth emanated from the forest.

The girls lining up in front of the meal distribution station seemed tired. They no longer had words or smiles. Soonboon got one lump of rice and pickled radish when her turn came. The smell of the grass and gunpowder melded together in the hot breeze. Over in the back of the barrack, white smoke rose as if something was burning. Soonboon headed back for the comfort station with Kumok. Thick shadows covered the station. Blue and white mold bloomed all around them like a carpet.

Knock, Knock. Soonboon knocked on Bongnyeo's room. There was still no movement. Soonboon drew the curtain and searched inside. Bongnyeo was lying on her side on the floor, not moving at all.

"It's me. You don't want to eat?"

Bongnyeo didn't answer her.

"Get up." Soonboon approached her, but she didn't move, showing her back to them. Kumok rushed to Bongnyeo and checked her face, worried by the silence.

"Are you sleeping?" Bongnyeo flattened her face into her pillow to avoid Kumok's eye contact. Kumok was relieved that she was alive.

"We brought dinner. Get up and let's share."

Soonboon took off a piece of her riceball and brought it to Bongnyeo's mouth, but she refused.

"Eat. You need to eat to stay alive. How many days are you going to act like this?" Soonboon said determinedly.

But if Soonboon pushed her more, Bongnyeo would turn her head away even further. Kumok looked at Bongnyeo, disheartened.

"You said let's run away. You need energy if you want to escape. How can you run away in this condition?" Soonboon asked argumentatively.

Bongnyeo finally looked at her. A sudden vigor flushed her eyes and then disappeared. Dried saliva stuck around her mouth. Soonboon helped her get up. The grueling Bongnyeo leaned against the wall and hardly looked at her, full of mixed emotions.

"You will be beaten if you are found here. Go back to your room."

"It's okay. They won't know, they are eating right now."

"Go back to your room, quickly."

"Then, drink this first."

Soonboon brought a water bowl near her mouth, then took a piece of rice ball and put it into her mouth. Bongnyeo hardly chewed.

"You should eat, so we can look toward the future again."

"I don't want to live."

"You said let's run away. We can only go together and I can't do it without you. Please stay alive and take me out of here. Eat."

Boongnyeo's eyes turned red and filled with tears.

"You'll get focused after you're done eating. We can survive, we can go home. No matter how hard it gets. This might not be the end. You said you want to study, you want to be a teacher. You will be a great teacher, you surely will. Let's survive. Make your dream come true. Please eat."

Although Soonboon said that she could make her dream come true if she survived, she was not sure whether it was actually possible. Bongnyeo looked at Soonboon as she spoke. Her eyes were depressingly blank. Soonboon took a piece and pushed it into Bongnyeo's mouth again.

"I want to see you become a teacher. I will be proud of you and brag to everyone that my friend is a teacher. Please eat and get some energy." Bongnyeo chewed the rice in her mouth slowly.

"Okay. Keep eating."

But Bongnyeo didn't eat much. After chewing several times, she turned her head aside.

"Eat some more."

"You eat," Bongnyeo pushed Soonboon and her lump of rice away.

"I am fine, you eat and don't worry about me."

"My stomach is upset."

"That's because you have not eaten for a couple of days. Eat slower."

Kumok, looking at the two girls, brought her bowl of water to Bongnyeo's mouth. After sipping a little water, Bongnyeo looked at the curtains worriedly.

"Hurry, go back to your room. You could be seen."

Soonboon was worried about the guard. They had no idea when they might come in.

"Go, you too, Kumok."

"Okay, don't think about anything. We will survive or die together. Don't forget that we can survive, together. Got it?"

Soonboon looked into Bongnyeo's eyes for confirmation, and Bongnyeo looked back at her slowly. Her eyes said she would do anything not to be here.

"Promise me," Soonboon hurriedly tried to persuade her.

"Okay. We will survive together or die together." Kumok aided Soonboon beside her.

Bongnyeo nodded her head after a while.

"I will be back at night if I can."

Soonboon laid Bongnyeo down on the floor and looked outside. A guard had already finished eating and was strolling around the comfort station. Soonboon and Kumok waited until he turned his back to go back to their rooms. Right after she got her breath back, a soldier entered. He must have rushed to eat and come to Soonboon right away. This one never failed to visit her. He was the one who called her Haruko.

"You are the best bitch, Haruko. Korean girls are better than Japanese girls. Do you know why I like it here? It is because of you, bitch, ha-ha-ha…" He opened her skirt, smirking unpleasantly. Soonboon hated that he called her Haruko. She wanted to shout that her name was Soonboon. Kim-Soonboon, the name that meant mild fragrance, the name that her father gave her, the name of a Korean, not a Japanese, not *Chosenjin*. *Although you call me Haruko, I will never be Haruko. I will always be Soonboon.* She reminded herself over and over.

Soonboon shut her eyes. When he slipped his throbbing dick into her genitals, she thought of the front mountain in her hometown and the stem of balsam flowers that bloomed under the fence of their straw house. She couldn't stand the smell of the soldiers, she never got used to it; it was the smell of death. The smell was a mix of gunpowder, blood, and sweat. These soldiers were living without knowing when they would die…That must have been why they were so vicious on top of the girls' bodies. They wanted to feel alive. Whenever his member entered her, her vagina ached. It was sore and bloodied, but the soldier didn't mind. Soonboon was disgusted. Then she heard a scream from the other room. *Rat-a-tat-tat…* There was the sound of somebody running and something being smashed. Who was it this time? Soonboon closed her eyes again. The butterfly fluttered into her closed eyes. *Flutter, flutter, flutter,* went the butterfly, looking like a large snowflake whose glistening edges quivered, beckoning Soonboon to touch it.

"Hurry up, hurry up."

The soldier outside of the curtain rushed the man panting on top of her body.

20. Time as an Animal

During intercourse with a soldier, Soonboon sometimes fell asleep for a while. Far away, she heard whistling, and the sound of people babbling. She had thought the sound was in her dream, but it was not. She perceived strange sounds between sleep and wakefulness. Another soldier was panting on top of her, sweat running down himself as though he had just gotten out of the shower. Soonboon woke up. *Thump, thump*. There were girls' footsteps, and screaming. The steps transmitted her back to where she was. She tried to open her eyes, but sleep clung to her eyelids. Girls' screams were heard again. The constant screams finally pulled her out from sleep. The soldier on top of her rushed to finish and went out to chase the screaming. She followed him to find the origin of the sound.

Soonboon couldn't believe her eyes. One girl was dead, an iron stick stuck in her genitals. The girl's eyes stared into space. What was the last thing this girl had seen? Was it the face of the soldier who killed her, or was it the black-ish wooden ceiling of the comfort station? It would be too cruel to have seen the soldier's face as he killed her.

"How did her..." Soonboon mumbled. Kumok approached her, pale-faced, and answered: "She had syphilis and transferred it to the officer without knowing, so the officer pushed a burning iron stick into her genitals." Soonboon was horrified. This was a truly horrible death. They couldn't do this even to animals... how could one do this to a person? When he pulled out the iron stick from her genitals, burning flesh adhered to the stick. The girls closed their eyes, looking away from this madness. Soonboon couldn't cry. Life is tenacious, but not for everyone. How could life be more vain than this? After watching the girl's death from the burning stick, the girls took out the condoms they had reserved to wash, stunned. They knew used condoms should be replaced, but there were not enough supplies during wartime. The only common supplies were the lives of people in colonial lands- the *Chosenjin*. The lives of Koreans were the most common supplies they could use, and dispose of.

Since the condoms were not enough, they were sold at a high price. For this reason, girls collected used ones and reused them after washing. A ripped and holed condom didn't perform its function, but the girls still didn't get rid of it. Throwing away a condom was like throwing away their lives. But the men often beat them when they took out their condoms. Wearing a condom was not fun for them. But when the diseases were transferred, they beat them even more.

"I got diseases from you dirty bitches. Dirty *Chosenjin*, you are a disgusting, nasty race."

They beat them for being dirty. Or for looking at the moon, wondering what they were thinking about. When the girls mumbled, they whipped them, accusing them of using swear words.

Kitanai, bakayaro... They repeated those words and beat the girls over and over. Soonboon imitated their words in spite of herself. *Kitanai, bakayaro, Kitanai, bakayaro...* Strangely those words slipped out of her mouth in the same pattern. *Kitanai*, Soonboon was dirty. The soldiers who came to her were dirty. *Bakayaro*, Soonboon was stupid. The soldiers were stupid. They were all living as animals: dirty and stupid. The comfort station was dirty, too. The moment was the dirtiest of all, dirtier than the reeking smell of moldy water under the summer sun.

21. Life, Segmented

Bongnyeo got back on her feet. She still had anger in her heart, but she didn't express it. Kumok, however, followed orders obediently as if she had given up. Soonboon woke up at the appointed time, had the three meals they provided, sometimes washed her clothes, and took a sitz bath when she could. She sometimes did the laundry and repaired soldiers' uniforms, following orders. Soonboon noticed some black spots on some uniforms as she washed them. She knew from a gut feeling what they were. It was blood that had circulated someone's body not long ago. *Throb, throb.* The heart had been healthy, and the blood was still hot. She didn't know whether this blood's owner was alive or dead. Blood ran like a stream on the battlefield. Soonboon did not feel afraid. She knew she herself was located at the border of life and death, living with one foot in this life, the other in death.

Soonboon felt a soreness and itching in her genital area. Sores oozed, and blood often came out mixed with her urine, smelling terrible. Soldiers still impatiently rushed the men before them, eager for their turn, not even giving her any time to wash her privates though she told them how much it hurt.

Soonboon waited for breakfast, hurried to finish her meal, and rushed to the restroom to take a sitz bath. When she lifted the curtain, other girls were in the baths, crouching and full of worries. There was no proper soap, only coarse salt. When she put the salt near her private parts, they burned with all the suffering the soldiers had caused. Tears flooded her eyes with the pain, but she had to overcome it. She was slightly comforted seeing that she wasn't the only girl with this disease. It was strange that something like this could give her condolence. Even in hell, perhaps, there could be something to comfort her. The fact that she was not alone, the fact that they all had the same disease: these consoled her a lot.

As she washed her private parts with salt, she thought that she should get a diagnosis. If they confirmed she had a venereal disease, they would allow her to turn over the name tag in front of her room. A turned over name tag meant soldiers should not use the room since the girl inside had a venereal disease, and this would let her rest a while. Getting a disease could sometimes be better than not having one—an uncertain time to rest which sometimes led to death—yet it was better than being raped by soldiers every day. If they were unlucky, some girls were killed for their venereal diseases, but either way, it was a matter of life or death. The soldiers realized that killing too many girls would be a disadvantage for them.

When she went out after her bath, the bell rang.

"Everyone, pay attention." Angry whistle sounds gathered all the girls. Girls in the restroom rushed to finish washing, dried their hands and went out. Their faces looked tired and full of worry about what bad things would happen this morning.

"What happened this time?"

"I don't know. Did somebody run away?"

Soonboon mingled among the throng of girls.

"Make a line, don't you know how to make a line? Make a row, stupid bitches! Don't you understand what I'm saying?"

Following the order, the girls quickly made a line, front to back. The bobbed-haired girls were led by abandoned expressions. Lacking all hope or desire, their faces were lifeless, inanimate. They had no expectations or desires for tomorrow, though they might have had dreams before. But their dreams had been destroyed, and now they lived as if they were objects or dead: it was another homicide.

Soonboon's eyes flew toward one of the girls. Her belly was prominent, and a soldier's whip lashed towards that part of her body. Exhausted, she was being pushed towards the man with the whip. The girl stood facing the other girls, and Soonboon could not look away from her abdomen. Something was inside of her. One of the soldiers approached her. His slanted eyes watched as the whip divided the morning sky. The long leather strap rolled across her body, and she fell to the floor with a bloody scream.

"What a stupid bitch. How many times have I told you to be careful not to conceive? Is pregnancy a prize? How dare you deny comforting the Imperial Japanese Army with the excuse of conceiving?"

Her belly looked more distinct as she placed her palm on the floor, attempting to stand.

"This is all your fault. We don't need the stupid bitch like you. We need dedicated girls who are better at personal hygiene."

He pointed out the girl with his chin to his subordinate.

"Take her."

Right after his order was given, his subordinate took the pregnant girl. She struggled not to go, but she couldn't overcome them.

"I will say it again. Your duty is to help the Great Japanese Army concentrate on the battle, to relieve their worries, as well as to please them and make them happy. Focus on your personal hygiene help let the soldiers lead healthy lives. I will never forgive you bitches if you deny comforting them because of pregnancy like her. Do you understand?" His speech was very long this time.

"All of you, come forward for your injection and medication."

His voice was like the cold black aim of a gun. It was confirmed again that death hovered right over their heads.

Bad news travels fast. There was a rumor spreading secretly that many soldiers had lost the will to fight since they had contracted syphilis. That was why they gave the girls injections although it was not the scheduled time to get them. The smell of this injection was stronger than the previous one. The odor filled their noses and fogged up the morning. The girls rolled up their sleeves and stood at the medical station. Soonboon waited her turn, pulling up her sleeves. When the needle stuck in her vein, she felt the liquid enter into her blood. It was so strong that Soonboon recoiled and felt the world fade to yellow. She liked this feeling better than how she normally felt. The shot relaxed her, and for once, she forgot her current worries. The soldier's vulgar language seemed to swirl around strangely, and his face lost its power in Soonboon's eyes.

Salvarsan 606 was its name. Having started at number one, 606 was the strongest medication yet. When she started to turn away, they called her back and gave her a white button-shaped tablet. One day Kumok explained as she put the white tablet on her palm: "Do you know what this is for? It's for shrinking the uterus. If you take this pill, it prevents you from conceiving."

Looking at the small tablet in her hand, Soonboon felt sad. Why did she miss the paulownia tree flower at that moment? The tree that stood tall in front of the high gate of a wealthy family in her hometown, with huge purple flowers, and lighting up the narrow alley in the spring. Soonboon had often been to the rich family's gate to visit the flowers. She stood in front of the paulownia tree and watched the flowers for many long hours. One spring day, she complained to her dad that he should plant a paulownia tree, but he didn't answer her, and continued to sprinkle balsam seeds under the fence. Soonboon realized later why they planted paulownia, why the paulownia flower bloomed brightly like a light at every house with daughters. When a girl was born, they planted the paulownia tree to make furniture for the daughter when she got married. But why didn't dad plant paulownia for her? When paulownia flowers fell down, it meant the tree was growing. When the petals fell down, and when the flowers bloomed again, the tree trunk gained another ring, getting thicker with all the memories of that year. Annual rings added on one by one and the trunk thickened. It would turn into beautiful furniture someday, and move far away to follow the newly married girl. The light purple flowers were sorrowful flowers now, which she would never see again.

"Did you take the tablet?"

Kumok's eyes were looking straight through the wall ahead of her. She was looking somewhere, but she didn't see anything. Soonboon shook her head silently at the question.

"Take it, take it, so they don't harm you. Otherwise, you might get in trouble."

Maybe Kumok was saying these words to herself. Her eyes were still penetrating the wall, her mind far away.

"What happened to the pregnant girl?" Soonboon asked.

"I heard that they cut the belly and took out the baby while she was conscious at some military station. In another station, a military doctor removed the uterus and used her body for medical experiments. They are all horrible," Kumok answered, mumbling to herself.

Soonboon shuddered. Goose bumps covered her body. She felt a chill down her back and legs in spite of the sticky humidity of the scalding summer day. Soonboon took the white tablet, swallowing it without water. The medicine would melt in her blood, drying up her body, making her infertile and unable to conceive. She might never have a baby in her whole life. Indeed, how could she dream of becoming pregnant with this dirty body? How could she think of any man, how could she accept him, and how could she dream of a normal married life? She might not ever be able to have an ordinary life as the woman she always dreamed she would be…

22. Infertile Body

Soonboon's privates didn't get any better. When it seemed like things were improving, pus would ooze out again and it got worse. No wonder it didn't get better, considering she would serve more than a dozen men every day. No, it would continue to be abnormal for this to be normal. Everything in this tropical country smelled musty, and this same mustiness rose from her lower body. It was as if everything were covered in decay; the earth was moldy from the sticky humid weather, the soldiers smelled stale, and even the washed, dry clothes were smelly.

Though they had their shots and pills, little lives still became fertilized in these infertile uteri. Pregnant women continued to serve the soldiers because the delivery of virgins had been slowing down for some time. As long as they didn't have a venereal disease, they should care for the Great East Asia War that the Imperial Japanese Army was now facing not for themselves. The girls thought that they were lucky if they could only survive.

As Soonboon washed the clothes one day, a pregnant girl caressed her big belly with a baby whose dad was unknown, and she mumbled to herself:

"You are so pitiful. How did you get into my un-promised body? Your life is the same as mine."

Her eyes were sad with love for the baby in her womb, one hand on her big belly and the other caressing the child who kicked her from inside. Motherhood still existed in this harsh time, making her feel sorrow and pity for the baby starting its life inside such a weak body. If she could deliver it and raise it, she would love the baby inside her, though it came from the seed of someone who had abused her.

When girls became pregnant, they were given very potent injections. After a few of them, blood discharged from their vaginas. Little fetuses ran down in red blood, never to be born into the world. However, some fetuses somehow survived, were born and cried for the first time. These babies were usually given the mom's maiden name since they never knew who the dad was.

It seemed like everything was melting under the hot sunlight. Faces burned red, and earthworms moved to the shadows to avoid the burning sun. Soonboon's disease got no better despite injections and the medicine she took. Once the virus settled in her body, it expanded throughout her and tormented her. Even if she washed with medicine from the clinic and scrubbed it with salt, it didn't heal. She couldn't survive if she had the venereal disease three times. One girl with pus from her pubis to her belly was taken somewhere, and the other girl who had transmitted her disease to the officer died from the iron stick he had stuck in her vagina.

Soonboon was afraid. Even though she turned over the name tag hanging outside her room, an impatient soldier who couldn't stand to wait in the long lines in front of the other rooms rushed into Soonboon's room. His military uniform was filled with dirt and sweat from his constant training. When the soldier entered her room, the odor spread toward her. She held her breath.

"Didn't you see the name tag was turned over?" Soonboon said, annoyed.

"Okay, so give me a blow job."

Soonboon scooted her butt back away from him.

"Do it with your mouth. Earn your keep."

The bad smell from his mouth gave her headache. He gripped her hair. Soonboon teared up, furious with pain like the skin was being peeled from her head. She grabbed his hands to release his grip.

"Please, let go, please…"

Instead of letting her go, he pulled her face to his groin and pushed his penis into her mouth. Soonboon tried to turn her head aside, but she couldn't overcome his force. His dick blocked her airway, and she couldn't breathe, but he didn't stop. He spun his waist as he gripped her hair and moved his penis back and forth in her mouth. Whenever his penis got very deep, she choked, feeling she would die soon. She struggled to escape from him. But if she fought, his hand would tighten even more. Someone lifted the curtain and watched him thrust his waist with his penis in her mouth, with an excited face and wicked smile.

Just then, the room turned into gloom and the wind was swirling in the darkness. Soonboon saw the white butterfly was captured by the wind, and tried to escape. "Butterfly, butterfly, fly up, up to the sky. Get out of there! Fly, fly up high. As high up as you can…" Soonboon yelled. But suddenly, a black hand came out from the darkness and grabbed the right wing of the butterfly. Soonboon clawed the air with both hands to escape from the man and go to help the butterfly. The butterfly was struggling to escape from the hand. But the more it struggled, the more its wing was torn inside of the hand. "Butterfly, fly, fly away from him. Get out of there. Please don't kill it. Please let it go, please…" Soonboon shouted. She cried. Then everything disappeared in an instant. Where had the butterfly gone? She closed her eyes, tearing up. Butterfly, butterfly, where are you? Where are you, butterfly, are you okay? Please don't die. please…

After the man pulled up his pants and left, the next son of a bitch came in and grabbed her hair. Gagh, gagh, Soonboon gagged from the penis in her mouth.

Whenever his penis got deep into her mouth, her gag reflex moved up her throat, but he was only concentrated on satisfying his sexual instinct. After he had spilled his warm seminal fluid in her mouth, he put on the pieces of his military uniform one by one and went out of the room. Soonboon spit it out over and over again, but his fleshy smell in her mouth never left. The curtain was lifted again, and another soldier came in. It was the Korean who she liked.

"Didn't you see the name tag was turned over?" Soonboon said, disobeying again. Soonboon had a strange feeling about him again. She felt like she wanted to urinate and she felt very sorry for him. She felt for the first time that she wanted to give her body to a man sincerely. She wanted to relieve the fatigue of his life even for a moment. Although he came into Soonboon's room, he didn't want her body. He just came and went back after taking a rest. She asked him once, "Why don't you do it when others are so crazy for it?"

"Anyhow both of us are tired, so when will we take a rest if not now?" He had answered, lying outstretched on his back with closed eyes.

Today, he started snoring low after lying down on the floor, having fallen asleep right away. The compulsory military-drafted Koreans were sent to the front lines, acting as human shields and bait. They also were not treated as feeling, living persons. They knew their fate more than anybody else. They were aware that they couldn't go back to their hometowns alive. In the presence of oncoming death, their emotions became empty, and dark. As they watched death coming towards them, they could almost touch it with their outstretched arms.

All of a sudden, he exhaled loudly and sprung up like a metal spring, looking around. He might have had a bad dream. What dreams made him wake up in turmoil? Soonboon noticed that the rims of his eyes looked collapsed. She wanted to ask what dream he had, but she couldn't. He swept his face with his hands as if washing it, then gave her a military ticket and rushed out. From behind he seemed in a flash of bewilderment.

23. Secret Conspiracy

Everything was dark without any light whatsoever. No, there was a light, a starlight that shone in a spot in the dark sky: *blink, blink*. The sky held pale moonlight. The bright stars and faded light slightly revealed the borders of objects.

Soonboon liked the darkness. She loved the soft moonlight and blinking stars that dispelled it. She felt cozy looking at the moon and starlight. This was a time when she didn't need to show her ugly self, the time when nobody was looking at her, not making her feel foolish or uncomfortable. But this was not allowed every day. Sometimes an officer stayed in her room during the whole night, not letting her sleep. He would harass her until twilight, as if the world would end if the sun rose. Whenever he touched her, sleep evaded her. Her body suffered the whole night, but she could never say she couldn't do it, and she couldn't whine about it, either.

She remembered what Kumok had said one day: "It happened at another military station. One day, the officer called the girls and asked them to raise their hands if they could serve one hundred soldiers in one night, and if they didn't raise their hands, they killed them all, saying they didn't need girls with rotten minds like that."

Soonboon couldn't believe it. "No way!"

"It's true. It actually happened. The officer who came to me last night told me the story like he was proud of it."

Soonboon couldn't believe it- she didn't want to. She just couldn't help getting goosebumps. Death was nothing new to them, so they were not sad and mournful anymore when girls disappeared or were killed. The soldiers just felt that removing the dead bodies was a burden. The deaths of girls just meant that more of their supplies were gone.

Soonboon held her hands together on her chest, lying down in the darkness. A sound triumphed over the darkness, getting louder in the dark. She heard the wind passing through the branches and the sound of anonymous birds chirping. She thought she heard the sound of someone weeping in a lower voice, mixed with the cry of insects. Who was it? Who was crying in this dark night? Heat didn't cool down even at night in this tropical country, but she was used to it now. Only sudden rain and dense tree leaves making shadows during the day removed the heat. But there was one thing that she couldn't tolerate, no matter how much time passed: the men who made a line and waited for their turn in front of the girls' rooms. She had abandoned every hope of returning to a normal, happy life, but still wished she could cut the soldiers' throats, watching them die on top of her body.

Soonboon hoped the sun wouldn't rise. How happy I could be if this dangerous and critical peace could continue! *Knock, knock.* The signal had arrived; it came from Bongnyeo's room. Soonboon answered—*knock, knock.* One knock meant someone was in the room. Two knocks said they were alone. No knock was terrible since it meant that someone was sleeping the whole night in their room.

Knock, knock.

Knock, knock.

The signal that came back and forth at night was quiet and secret. Bongnyeo came to Soonboon's room like black charcoal moving in the darkness. Soonboon stood up and made space for her.

"Come on."

Their two shadows were dim under the infiltrating moonlight. Kumok came over to Soonboon's room rapidly as if she had heard their signals.

"I am here, too." They left their bodies under the gentle moonlight.

"How about your body? Is it getting better? I am worried about it, it shouldn't take so long to get better."

"I can't stand it anymore."

Kumok had asked Soonboon and now Bongnyeo spoke. Bongnyeo's voice sounded determined. Soonboon couldn't say anything to her resolute voice.

"I'd rather die, I can't take it anymore."

"We don't know yet where to go after getting out of here, plus we don't speak the local language here, so how can we go?" Soonboon let out a deep sigh, holding her knees. Kumok wiggled her toes, and they flashed under the moonlight as she listened to their conversation. The soft moonlight revealed the back of her feet and toes.

"What's the difference whether we stay here or die outside? If I stay here longer, the humiliation will only get deeper. I will escape. How about you?" Bongnyeo asked Soonboon.

"I will escape, too. I should go, but it is not the right time."

"There is no perfect time. How about you?" Bongnyeo asked Kumok this time.

"…Don't know, I, I don't know," Kumok answered timidly.

She was still, wiggling her toes under the moonlight. It seemed like her toes were tickled by the moon. Nobody said anything after that. Only the moon spoke subtly in this quiet place, beckoning them.

"So? When do you want to escape? You don't mean right now, do you?" Soonboon started to talk again.

"Now is not a bad time."

"I am scared," Kumok mumbled to herself while looking down at her toes.

"Then, let's get out of here when the next air-raid siren rings. Let's escape together then. We should start preparing now… but, if… if we make it, are you going to go back to your hometown?" Soonboon asked, but Bongnyeo didn't answer.

Soonboon knew what it meant when she didn't answer. It was the place where they wanted to go, but couldn't. It was the only place they wished to go back to, but they were scared to.

Bongnyeo had a reason to go back to her hometown. Soonboon and Kumok had reasons to go back as well. Soonboon had a family there, Kumok had a sister whom she should take care of. Soonboon had parents whom she should rescue from the impoverishment choking them like shackles. Bongnyeo wished to study to be a teacher; she wanted to lead a better life.

Soonboon touched the remaining wounds on her body. The wounds on her chest and palms made rice cake patterns, neither healed nor hidden. They approached Soonboon in her dreams like a big snake and choked her.

"Surveillance is getting tighter when the siren wails. You saw that they have emergency mount guards so it will be harder to run away. We should wait until they are not at attention. Otherwise, we could run away when going to the clinic," Bongnyeo said while looking at the leaves in the moonlight, the moon gently sat on the leaves.

"How about you? What do you want to do? Do you want to stay here or go with us?" Bongnyeo asked Kumok this time.

"I don't know," Kumok answered hesitantly, her knees pulled in and held with both hands, her chin resting on them.

"Soonboon and I will escape, do you want to stay here by yourself?"

Kumok didn't answer, she sobbed instead.

It was strange. Soonboon's heart pounded when she thought about getting out of here. Anxiety, excitement, and fear mingled and made her fret. With the thoughts of running away, Soonboon felt that this night was different from previous nights. Just then, a whistle sounded, echoing across the thick darkness. The noise seemed sharper and more rambunctious at night when all other sounds had disappeared.

"You could be detected, go back to your rooms." Soonboon lifted the curtain and watched the movements outside, rushing Bongnyeo and Kumok out. They went back to their rooms, moving on muffled tiptoe. Before Soonboon could catch her breath, a soldier roughly drew the curtain and came in. It was the officer who always visited Soonboon, and the sound of the whistle meant the air-raid was cleared.

24. Expanding the Battle Line

The pitch-black darkness was gone, and bluish daybreak ascended quietly. Soonboon woke up and saw the dawn ripen and turn to bright daylight. The soldier who came to her last night was sleeping and snoring. Soonboon wondered, how was it for them, feeling their deaths being delayed day by day? The shadow of death existed not only among the girls at the comfort station but also among the surviving soldiers. Their expressions were blank instead of joyful; they didn't know what would happen next time though they had survived this time. Some got furious at small things, others just looked on with folded arms. Others became obsessed with minor things. This was all because of death's constant hovering around them. Everyone was trying to find a way to survive.

Soonboon moved back, shrinking her body down in case the man touched her. No matter how many men had raped her body, she never got used it. When they touched her, she still shuddered as if a cold blanket had been thrown on her. *I will run away. I can't stay here anymore.* She remembered what Bongnyeo had said. *I should go. If Bongnyeo escapes, I will go with her. What exists outside of the comfort station? What will be waiting for us? It will be better than living here as a sex slave.* It will be better than staying here where she couldn't stop having intercourse although her organs twisted and her vagina ached so much she couldn't even sit on it. It would be better to escape, even if she needed to eat grass roots and tree bark. Soonboon bit her lower lip hard.

If I get out of here, if I succeed, can I go back home? Will I be able to see mom and dad if I go back? Can I bring snack to my parents working in the field and chase butterflies again in the warm spring field? Will it still be possible to get married and have babies one day?

Her thoughts about escaping the comfort station and what would happen after that, swirling around in her head and awaken her consciousness. The bluish dawn became thin, starting to reveal the shapes and colors of objects. She heard barking and chirping sounds from far away. They were unknown birds in the trees. The soldier who had greedily desired her body last night trembled and jerked. His forehead wrinkled fiercely as if he were in a nightmare, and the corners of his mouth twitched as he talked in his sleep.

"Kill everybody. Don't value your life over your great country. The country will think you are a hero, so go and fight. Don't be afraid of death."

It seemed he was battling his enemies in his dream. He might be aiming a gun to kill an enemy with bloodshot eyes, knowing full well he would be killed if he didn't kill them first. Maybe he would cut the enemy's neck with his sword... Tears ran down from his eyes, and Soonboon looked at him with sympathy. Soonboon touched his tears and tried to wipe them, but he suddenly opened his eyes and clasped her wrists instinctively.

"Ouch, it hurts!" Soonboon screamed and grabbed her gripped wrist with her other hand. He looked around as she cried and frowned, noticing where he was.

"How dare you, bitch! How dare you touch my face?"

He knitted his brows and twisted her arms as the cruel words leaked through his teeth.

"It hurts. I was just wiping your tears since you were crying in your dream," Soonboon said, groaning in pain. He rubbed his eyes and stared at her, then released her arm and put back on his military uniform. Her arm throbbed with pain.

The next morning, the heat was intense. The cicadas sang loudly, competing to find mates. The sound caused a ringing in her ears. The conspiracies of last night with Bongnyeo gave her new energy. She could tolerate any assault, contempt, or humiliation, today thanks to the revitalized plot of Soonboon and her friends. Soonboon finished cleaning her room and went to the well to wash some clothes, but she couldn't do it. She was still feeling a sharp pain in her wrist.

"Since my wrist was swollen, I couldn't wash the clothes." She showed her swollen wrist to the guard. He looked at it, doubting at first but then confirmed it and said, "Fine, then you can sew."

Soonboon took one of the uniforms from the basket. The mood inside the military station was disordered and different from other days. The trucks delivering supplies came in and out of the barracks diligently, and soldiers came and went, armed. The business of the morning today was unusual. What had happened? Soonboon looked at them while stringing a needle, and over-heard what they were saying: new troops had come near them since the battle line was being expanded. *The battle line has been expanded?* They didn't say whether this was a disadvantage or an advantage for them. Perhaps they might not know, or they didn't want to mention it even though they knew. Every-thing was secretive: the location of the military base, and the names of the troops. All should be a secret. The girls should not know, and they should not try to understand.

Soonboon's heart pounded unevenly. She didn't know whether Japan was winning or losing. What would happen to them if Japan lost the war? *Can I go back? What will they do with us? Otherwise, if Japan wins, then what will happen to us?* She felt a sharp pain in her finger. Soonboon screamed without meaning to. The needle had poked her fingertip, blood coming out and forming a drop. Soonboon put it into her mouth and sucked the blood out.

Just then, a naked girl was dragged out of the room by her hair. She was the Korean girl who had been at the comfort station before Soonboon arrived. Her screams and curses broke the peace of the morning. Soonboon wanted to run away from the screams and curses, from this moment. The soldier holding the girl's hair bumped her head hard against the floor. *Bam! Bam!*

All of a sudden, Soonboon's back was struck by something.

"What are you doing, lazy bitch?" The guard came to her and lashed a whip across her back. *Chik! Crak!* The whip flew through the air, striking her body and opening her flesh. At the start, she had only felt irritation, but now the wounds caused by the whip were sore and painful. The strap ripped at her clothes, and blood spewed out from her soft flesh. Soonboon rushed to sew a fallen button.

"These bitches do nothing if they are not beaten. We should never believe *Chosenjin*," he yelled, clenching his teeth and glaring toward the girls.

Now Soonboon felt pain in her back, wrist, and finger. It seemed there would be no relief. Soonboon's head remained twisted up with thoughts of what the soldiers had said a while ago: if new troops had come to the area, then how many more soldiers would there be to harass the girls?

The naked girl was dragged back to her room, still alive.

25. The Legend of a Star

Before she knew it, stars had settled down near the earth. The sky was still beautiful even when the world was not. The stars looked like broken glass in the sky that night, glittering with flecks of blue, the Milky Way passing through the middle of the sky within the haze of starry clouds. The stars were bright one day, and dark the next. The stars hid one day and showed their bright faces the next. *Perhaps people become stars when they die*, Soonboon thought. Although their bodies would be buried, rotting in the earth, their souls would fly up to the sky, turning into the different colored stars, and then they will illuminate the night, whispering to the people on earth.

When her mom heard that one of her relatives died, she had shed a lot of tears. She cried and cried until her skirt was wet from wiping her tears, but she didn't stop crying then. Her eyes were swollen from crying. Soonboon had never seen the relative; she just heard that the dead relative was on mom's side and that he liked mom a lot when she was younger.

Women were no longer a member of their own family after getting married, and it was a virtue that women should be ghosts of their in-laws' family after dying. But she didn't forget the relatives from her own family because blood is thicker than water. When she heard that her uncle died after a long, drawn-out illness without having enough water to drink, she said confidently, "I saw it, I saw it precisely with my eyes. When I stepped down into the yard, I saw a blue spark fly up to the sky suddenly. I was wondering what it was, but it was uncle's soul. The blue spark danced like a firefly, then it leaped up to the sky, and disappeared. The blue spark light was like starlight."

Mom believed that her uncle's soul had become a star. Like mom said, if each star was someone's life once, it might be the soul of a dead person. So, had the girls who died suddenly become stars shining somewhere in the sky? Soonboon didn't want to become a star when she died. She didn't want to leave any trace that she existed in this world. She wanted her assaulted body to disappear without a trace, vanishing from peoples' memories: this was Soonboon's desire of death that helped her to survive. Warm tears flowed down from her eyes.

A beating sound came from Kumok's room as if a soldier had come to sleep there. "Bitch, beg to save yourself. Beg me to save you. Dirty whore, dirty *Chosenjin*." His words cut out intermittently as a result of his shortness of breath. Slapping sounds mixed in like a chorus as he beat Kumok. Whenever the man's words ended, Kumok cried out saying help me, save me. Strangely it looked, out Soonboon's window, like the stars blinked whenever Kumok asked him to save her. *Come here, little girl.* It sounded like the stars answered Kumok: *Don't cry, come here, we will save you.* This fourteen year-old girl, once beautiful and innocent, in full bloom, had lost her way on the road, the very same path Soonboon had been on.

Knock, knock. Bongnyeo sent a signal. *Knock, knock.* Soonboon responded. Bongnyeo lifted the curtain and came over right away.

"How is your wrist?" Bongnyeo asked, catching a glimpse of it.

"Much better."

Bam! Bam! "Bitch. I can kill you anytime. Your life is in my hands." *Bam! Bam!* "So you should be a good girl to me. Be nicer." *Bam! Bam!*

"Save me, don't kill me."

"Louder, beg me louder."

"Save me. Please help me, don't kill me, save me, PLEASE!"

The sound of the soldier's carnal desires being satisfied was regularly heard from Kumok's room. The weak veneer wall shook, the *tatami* floor creaked. Bongnyeo covered her ears with her palms and tried to escape from the sounds, but they snuggled closer to her, suffocating under the dense and humid night air. The sound wasn't only coming from Kumok's room. Soldiers who couldn't know if they would live tomorrow came into the girls' rooms to seek solace in the night. Each day they survived in the battlefield, they became beasts in the night to prove that they were still alive.

"New troops will come," Soonboon said. Bongnyeo didn't say anything about it. She knew if new troops came, this would mean they would need to serve more soldiers. The sounds from Kumok's room continued without ceasing. Bongnyeo blocked her ears with her palms and shook her head in an attempt not to hear. Her face distorted with anger and pain. *Bam! Bam!* "I will kill you, I will kill you." *Bam! Bam! Bam!* "Please help me, save me." *Bam! Bam! Ahhh…*

Soonboon stared at a spot on the wall. No order could be found in this place. Only thick darkness, and confusion. Some girls tolerated it like they had given up on their lives, some remained as spectators like flies on the wall, yet some girls still resisted, unbroken.

The reward of resistance was often death. Most girls just lived because they were not yet dead, and they woke up because their eyes still opened every morning.

"I will run away within a couple of days," Bongnyeo said, determined.

"You don't know the geography of this area…"

"Even if I get caught running away, it would be better than living here. Dying is better than living here like this."

Bongnyeo's voice was resolute, and there was no hesitance, as if she was already made up her mind.

"How about you? Do you really want to go with me?"

Soonboon couldn't answer without more serious consideration. She wanted to run away with her, but she was not ready yet. She should not carry out dangerous plans based on a feeling. They had to succeed in one attempt, precisely and perfectly without fail. There were no second chances. They needed to prepare perfectly, with detailed attention paid to every move. It seemed like there was not enough time to prepare for it. She needed a couple of days more to be ready in her mind as well. Bongnyeo muttered to herself since Soonboon didn't answer.

"I will go by myself if you don't go." Her voice was even more determined.

"I don't mean I am not going. I'm just worried about time. We need more time to prepare."

"Then, when? When will you be ready? I can't tolerate it anymore. It is hell in here. I'd rather die than live here," Bongnyeo shouted in a lower voice as if arguing.

"Right, me too…" Soonboon mumbled to herself.

26. Condom, Cookies, Blouse

Rinnng, rinnng, the bell for breakfast distribution tolled.

Soonboon drew the curtain and went outside. This morning looked different since she was thinking about how she would escape the comfort station within a few short days. The air seeping into her nose felt unusual and so did the color of the morning. People looked different, and the trees looked different. Not just the world seemed odd, but also the blood circulating her body moved faster than other days. She was nervous for her pounding heart, reacted sensitively to little sounds, and was concerned about even minor changes in people's facial expressions.

She was self-conscious about her change in attitude but she tried not to show it. She should spend her remaining time acting the same as the other days. Everything would be in vain if they noticed her secret plan. Even if she had promised to go with, she was afraid and was still worried about not having enough time to prepare their escape. On second thought, like Bongnyeo said, dying here would be the same as dying while trying to run away. *I want to flee from this hell as soon as possible. I will escape before I am ruined even more.* Bongnyeo's voice hovered around her ears. Right, it was the same to die here as dying running away. It would be better to escape with Bongnyeo rather than die here fruitlessly.

Riiing, briiing. The flippant bell rang again. A snakelike line formed in front of the meal distribution station. They ate to survive and to store nutrients in their bodies for tomorrow. Soonboon stood at the end of the line.

"Hey, hey."

She heard someone calling her from behind. Soonboon turned back toward the voice. A girl waved to her without coming out from her room even though the ringing had notified them of breakfast distribution. She had arrived at the comfort station before Soonboon had. She had given advice to Soonboon up on her arrival, telling her to do whatever the soldiers said. She had pitied and felt sorry for Soonboon. Then, she had asked how Soonboon had been taken, looking at her sorrowfully. Soonboon confirmed with her eyes that she had heard when the girl called out to her. The girl nodded, looking around, and waved her hand. Her face was the color of yellow gardenia seeds. Soonboon went to the girl's room, seeing that the line had not decreased. The girl was holding something out when Soonboon entered her room.

"You take it. You can wash the condom and reuse it. It is better than not using one."

She handed over the used condom and a set of clothes.

"How about you? What are you going to do without them?"

She smiled at Soonboon.

"I won't need it anymore."

"Why, why you don't need it?"

"I am leaving."

"Leaving?" Soonboon was shocked, wondering where she would be off to.

"Anyhow, I don't need it now, so you take it."

Soonboon didn't understand what she said and why she said it. She might have a plan in mind. What was it then? Was she transferring to another station or escaping like Bongnyeo? But she couldn't ask, everybody had a secret which should be protected and not be revealed. This was the way to save their lives, the only way to secure a sense of safety. "Eat this, too."

She took out two bags of cookies from her things and gave them to her. Soonboon felt uncomfortable, so she didn't take them immediately, feeling leery.

"Are you really giving me all these? What are you going to do without them?"

"Don't worry." She smiled. The smile seemed dangerous.

"Take it, and hide it before they notice it."

She forced Soonboon out. Soonboon went back to her room, holding all the stuff she had received, and opened it after coming back to her room. A white blouse had faded to the color of gardenia seeds but was like new, and below it, she saw a skirt. Almost one year had passed since Soonboon came here and she was still wearing the same clothing she was provided at her arrival.

After that, she had never received any clothes and never had a chance to prepare any new clothes either.

Soonboon touched the blouse she had received over and over again. The clothes weren't mended or torn, and were as graceful as butterfly wings. She wanted to take off her clothes that were stained with saliva and dried sperm. She wanted to change into the new blouse, but it was too valuable to wear right now. She wondered when she could wear this kind of clothing in this horrible place, wishing to wear them every single day. Soonboon decided to wear the outfit when she would leave the comfort station. Her happiness actually made her lunch taste good that day. A soldier suddenly rushed into her room before lunch ended and Soonboon hid the clothes behind her back.

"What are you hiding?"

His eyes glared doubtfully. Soonboon moved back and grabbed the clothes tightly. He forced her arms out and looked at the clothes that she had hidden.

"Aren't those clothes?"

He tried to grab them with outstretched arms, and Soonboon endeavored to block him, but he was stubborn to take them. Finally, he deprived them of her and looked back and forth between them and Soonboon suspiciously.

"No, please give them back."

"Why do you need these things?"

"Please give them back."

"Why do you need this bullshit? Why do you need such clothes? Your current clothes are sufficient to make soldiers happy."

"Please!"

He showed a wicked smile and struck the clothes with his sword. They were ripped into two pieces and fell to the floor. Soonboon picked up the clothes and cast a sidelong glance at him, eyes full of blame. The angrier her eyes were, the more wicked his smile got.

"You don't need this bullshit. Look at the monkeys over there. Do they wear any clothes? You are no different from them."

There were monkeys where he pointed outside. The mother monkey was sitting on a branch, her swollen right breast was red and drooping. Baby monkeys jumped around from branch to branch around their mother. Same as the monkeys...

He took off his pants and pushed Soonboon back. Needless to say, he rode on top of her body pushing his erection forward into Soonboon's body. There was nothing she could do right now except abandon herself. Soonboon knew that she would be killed if she pushed him away.

Another girl was dead from her genitals and nipples cut up, having disobeyed them. Her life was tenacious, she was still breathing as parts of her body were maimed. But the breathing didn't last long. They cut her neck after that, the sword boasting as it struck her. Soonboon and the other girls were too afraid to scream as they watched. The dead were being replaced by new girls coming in. Now they would all have to confront death someday like that nameless girl.

"I like you. I like your young, smooth flesh, it makes me crazy. Got it? You don't need that kind of clothing, you only need to think about how you can make soldiers happy. Starting with me, right now."

He talked while he was panting on top of her. Whenever he spoke, Soonboon despised the bad breath from his mouth. But he put his tongue into her mouth deeply searching everywhere, or bit her lips and hit her. Soonboon wanted to bite his tongue whenever it searched through her mouth, but she just barely stopped herself. He didn't let her go quickly. It seemed he had decided to enjoy his given time as much as possible. Her genitals, entwined with his, were sore and painful. She felt like her organs were detached and her uterus distorted. Soonboon let out a big groan in spite of herself, but he didn't care. The more pain she felt, the more he violated her. The world was shaking. She was confused if it was her body or the world, but she was sure that her life was quivering. A flower-like fifteen-year-old girl, a life that should have been holy and pure was trembling and being ruined from humiliation. After he had ejaculated on Soonboon's breast, he laid down outstretched on his back. When he was down on his back, letting out short breaths, Soonboon wanted to pull out his sword and slash his neck with it. She trembled trying to tolerate the impulse.

Just then, the curtain was lifted, and another soldier came in. The first one went out, hanging his uniform on his arm without finishing putting them on, and the new soldier reached her before she could wash her privates.

"Dirty. What a nasty bitch!" He touched Soonboon's body, still covered with the previous soldier's sperm, body smell, and saliva. Then he spat on her chest while saying she was dirty, and beat her. Whenever his rough hands touched Soonboon's body, she let out a low groan.

"*Chosenjins* are dirty, dirty *Chosenjin*."

Soonboon clenched her teeth. Let me close my eyes, I'd better close my eyes and run away. She closed them tightly. Inside her closed eyes, the world scattered into white dots and gathered again into a small speck. The speck moved up and down, back and forth and transformed into her butterfly. The butterfly fluttered its strong white wings inside her closed eyes. *Butterfly, butterfly! Please take me where you are going. Butterfly, butterfly, where are you? Please, take me where you are. I envy you for being able to go anywhere with your wings. You could cross the ocean and fly over the mountains. You could go to my mom. Please cross the ocean, fly over the mountains and take me to my dad. Butterfly, butterfly, give me your wings. I want to flutter, flutter... cast off the shell of my body and fly into the bright air.*

After his body shivered with the orgasm, he threw a brown military ticket at her as if giving her alms, then walked out her room. The ticket flew like the butterfly that she had met just now. But Soonboon's face distorted, realizing again that it was not.

The girls received a ticket each time their bodies were disgraced; it was another form of humiliation. They were useless, and would be deserted in vain. The numbers of tickets were only for evidence of the assaults and violations on their bodies, and the number represented the exact number of times they each wanted to die. The military ticket price was different for each class of soldiers. A ticket from a lower-ranking soldier was worth 1.5 won, 2 wons for non-commissioned officers, 2.5 wons for commissioned officers, and it cost three or four wons for spending the whole night. The soldiers didn't control their tickets well. In the beginning, the Japanese supervisor held all the tickets, but now that he was nowhere to be seen, they were controlled by the army. For this reason, the military tickets had no meaning at all.

Just then, someone's scream flew out, cutting through the afternoon heat, followed by a buzzing sound. What happened? Soonboon crawled out to look outside, then watched the scene with an absent expression. It was her, surely it was her- the girl who gave Soonboon the blouse, condom and two bags of cookies.

Her dead body was being dragged from her room. Her eyes bulged, her swollen face turned purple. It was not the face of someone who had lived just until yesterday. Her body was dragged by the arms as they brought her down the stairs. The soldier who dragged her spat, kicked, and cursed at her as though he was very annoyed. Soonboon shuddered at this scene, where death got no condolence or sympathy.

Eat it. Soonboon remembered her bright eyes as the girl had handed over the bag of cookies. On second thought, the eyes were full of abandon. But it would be better to say that they were shining from excitement than from abandon. Soonboon thought her eyes were simply tamed and trained. Her own eyes might be the same someday, on the day when she looks at this work as nothing, on the day when she finally can tolerate this kind of work without much pain. But… but how long did she need to wait to get used it? Soonboon had thought this as she received the cookies, condom, and new clothes from the girl. But this would not be so: her eyes were not the eyes of abandon.

Soonboon couldn't see the dead body anymore, so she came back to her room and breathed in and out deeply, hugging her knees to her chest. She was rather jealous of the girl's new found freedom. She envied her of moving on to a new world, escaping restriction, suppression, and humiliation.

She heard some fighting sounds coming from Bongnyeo's room, which soon turned into curses.

"What is this bitch doing here? Are you crazy, do you want to be just like that dead girl? Don't you know you should obey my orders as long as you stay here? Do you want to feel what death is like?"

A dull thud was heard in Soonboon's room as if he had kicked Bongnyeo, but there was no scream or response from her. Maybe she was doggedly tolerating it through clenched teeth. *I will run away from here:* she might be thinking. *Will everything return to normal if I go back home? The life that I had before coming here like nothing happened, like that…* While Soonboon was thinking about Bongnyeo's possible thoughts, the beating continued emanating from her room. *Can I look at mom's and dad's faces, smiling in delight? Can I dream of marrying an unknown man and preparing for the future?*

"This *Chosenjin*, die, die, die… The comfort station is fine without you. I don't need a bitch who doesn't listen to me."

Soonboon covered her ears with her hands and put her face against her knees to block the sounds. The kicking and cursing from Bongnyeo's room had stopped now, and there were just the sounds of a man's swift and regular movements along with rapid moans and deep breathing.

Soonboon took out the bag of cookies and fiddled with them. *Should I scatter them on the road to Hades? I'd better throw them to prevent her from starving since she doesn't have any money on the road for the afterlife.* What a pitiful life she had! How could she end her life so vainly, for the reason of being born as a colonial's daughter? Then she wrapped the cookies back up with torn pieces of clothes and hid them.

27. Conspire to Escape

Knock, knock. Bongnyeo sent a signal.

Knock, knock. Soonboon responded with the same sound. She was still alive. Bongnyeo came over to Soonboon's room immediately after sending a signal. Soonboon knocked on Kumok's room as soon as Bongnyeo had arrived, but there was no response from her. Maybe an officer was staying with her that night, in which case they should try not to be noticed by him. Bongnyeo and Soonboon moved over to Bongnyeo's room secretly, fearing that their sounds would leak over to Kumok's room. Bongnyeo's bruised and swollen eyes were revealed clearly under the moonlight when they arrived at her room.

"What happened to your eyes?"

Soonboon brought Bongnyeo under the golden candlelight and looked all around her face. At first, she twisted her face away to hide it, but soon she let Soonboon examine her. Bruises were not only around her eyes, but also on her calf, a smudge shaped peony blossom on her thigh, and black and blue marks on her back, further evidence of the beating. The bruises bloomed like spring flowers on her back. Soonboon comforted Bongnyeo as she looked back and forth at her face and the bruises.

"That must hurt."

"I can't stay here anymore," Bongnyeo answered immediately as if she had been waiting for Soonboon to speak.

"So what will you do?"

"I will escape tomorrow."

"Tomorrow?"

"Dying here is the same as dying outside, so I'd better die outside."

Bongnyeo's voice was resolute than usual.

"So what are you going to do? You said you would go with me. What do you want to do? Do you really want to go with me?" Bongnyeo looked at her decisively, her eyes urging for a quick answer. Soonboon couldn't answer so directly, though. She should get out of here, but she was afraid. She should go, but she didn't want to go. *If we escape, escape from here, then what will be waiting for us?*

"If you don't want to, I will escape by myself," Bongnyeo said, her eyes withdrawing.

Soonboon answered while hugging her knees with her arms and cupping her chin in them, "Does it have to be tomorrow?"

Soonboon asked as if for confirmation, and Bongnyeo answered clearly while looking at her.

"Yes, it has to be tomorrow. I will escape tomorrow."

Bongnyeo eyed Soonboon expectantly. Soonboon looked at her eyes for a while; they were firmer and more intense than usual. Her eyes were clear even in the darkness. Soonboon knew that her decision was unchangeable by any persuasion. She only had two options: leave with her or stay here alone.

"I will go with you."

"Are you sure? Do you really want to go with me?" Bongnyeo asked over and over again as if she couldn't believe her decision, or couldn't believe her ears. Soonboon hadn't really made her mind up yet, though she had said yes. She was frightened of the outside world. But if she didn't escape with Bongnyeo, she would live like an animal, as a shield for their sperm, for the rest of her life and die doing it. She was more scared by this.

"How about Kumok? What will we do with Kumok?" Soonboon looked toward Kumok's room worriedly.

"I will figure it out."

"When?"

"Breakfast time tomorrow."

"When are you going to escape?" Soonboon lowered her voice, even more, she was afraid it would leak into Kumok's room.

"I will leave right in the morning, after having breakfast. So, you should not be far from me. We will leave when they aren't paying attention."

"What should I prepare?"

"There is nothing to prepare, we don't have anything."

"Don't you think we have to prepare any food?"

"No, we can eat anything, grasses and trees are everywhere."

Soonboon was anxious.

"What will happen to us? Can we make it?"

Bongnyeo didn't answer this last question, and her not having an answer made Soonboon full of gloom.

The stars shone dazzlingly in the night sky. They were listening to Bongnyeo and Soonboon's conversation. The stars babbled amongst themselves, they were conspiring with the stars, encouraging the stars, and receiving comfort from the stars. Everything will be real tomorrow. Either I die or I live. Tomorrow will be an end and a beginning; most importantly the miserable life in here, this life as a sex slave… will be over.

I will die if I have to, I will live if I have to. Wherever I go, it will be better than living here like an animal. As she thought of tomorrow's escape, Soonboon felt new blood was being formed in her heart. It was neither excitement nor anxiety. A cool and fresh feeling circulated inside her body.

Soonboon went back to her room. While she lay down on the square space that was enough for only two people, recollections came to her in waves. She remembered when she chased the butterfly in her parents' field, and when she tolerated the heavy dust of the straw bundles: all these memories were brought back to her as if they happened yesterday. It was strange that the memories were reproduced so vividly. They were repeated without any missing parts, without distortion, consecutively, and in detail. Daily things she hadn't cared that much about at the time were remembered so fondly now. Things that had not been understood, or that she was indifferent about, were all held affectionately now, in her heart. *But where can I go after escaping here? Can I ever have that dream like I used to when I wished to live like my mom and sister?* Soonboon shook her head as she arrived that thought. Wherever she would go, it would be better than here, and then she could make a plan for the future.

But, wait, what is that? Soonboon chased a fluttering object in the air with her eyes. What was this glittering object that seemed like a shining spot in the starlight, the thing that shined blue, yellow, white, and then turned to black under the darkness? *What is that?* Soonboon's eyes followed the spot that changed colors. She followed it… it was a butterfly again, her butterfly. Soonboon stretched out her arms to catch it. Her hands danced in the air, but the butterfly flew mischievously away. *It's okay. It's fine if you come back to me again.* Soonboon smiled softly.

28. Kumok

Soonboon opened her eyes, startled. She must have fallen asleep. The sharp, bright morning sun was shining in her room instead of the starlight, and the morning was resolute and nervous. It was a morning like the others, but different. The color of the sunshine was strange. If the color on other mornings was golden, the color today was sharp, and cold like metal.

Soonboon searched for last night's butterfly. *Butterfly, butterfly, where are you? Are you still here?* She searched in all directions, but the butterfly was not to be seen anywhere in her room. Butterfly shining with all colors, butterfly transforming with all shades was gone. Soonboon could hear only the sound of her heart pounding. *Throb! Throb!* Her heart resounded loudly in her ears. *Throb! Throb!*

After swiftly cleaning her room, she followed the line for meal distribution and stayed apart in the back in case someone noticed her abnormal heartbeat. Then someone approached her- it was Bongnyeo.

Soonboon asked, "What about Kumok? Did you ask Kumok?

"Not yet." Soonboon and Bongnyeo avoided making eye contact and ventriloquized her speech. Soonboon looked around for Kumok, but didn't find her anywhere in the long line.

"I can't see Kumok. Is she still sleeping? Should I go get her?" Soonboon looked back to Kumok's room nervously.

"There might still be someone in the room," Bongnyeo answered in a low voice, her face looking unusually calm. Soonboon knew that her unusual face was a camouflage. Just then, Kumok came out of her room with a big yawn, an officer coming out as well: Kanemura. The epaulet on his shoulder was prominent on the background fabric. He was notorious for being cruel among the girls. He requested the girls to do it exactly the same way in the pornography book that contained the scene of intercourse. He was an insane man who only orgasmed while beating the girls. He drew a tattoo on one girl's body that could never be removed. They were signs and symbols and started from her genitals, went up past her belly, neck, face and finally ended at her tongue. Soonboon couldn't breathe just from the sight of him.

Kumok didn't come to the meal distribution area right away, but stayed to enjoy the sunshine under the eaves. Her face still seemed sleepy. She was swaying while swaying her arms and neck. The sun passed by, casting a shadow on her face. Kanemura might not have allowed Kumok to sleep during the whole night. Why the hell was it so important to do that?

"Can I get her?" Soonboon asked with her eyes.

"Let's leave her alone," Bongnyeo answered with her eyes as well.

The meal distribution line shortened and Bongnyeo waited for Soonboon after she received her meal. She walked ahead, Soonboon following her. Bongnyeo went over to Kumok. She was slumped down on the floor under the eaves. Bongnyeo was surprised and ran over to her, putting aside her bowl of rice. Soonboon felt all her power leaving her legs.

"Hey, Kumok, Kumok," Bongnyeo shook her shoulders.

Kumok opened her eyes faintly in response, she was not dead. Soonboon was relieved to see she was alive, but Kumok was shaken only weakly by Bongnyeo's hands.

"Kumok, wake up, wake up," Bongnyeo called to her in a rough voice.

Thwack! She slapped her cheek, but Kumok avoided her and moved her face to the side, annoyed, but her gestures were still abnormal. Bongnyeo grimaced her face angrily.

"What's going on? Is she sleeping?" Soonboon asked while looking back and forth at Bongnyeo and Kumok. Soonboon had a dark thought at that moment.

"Is she sleeping?" Soonboon asked again since Bongnyeo didn't answer.

"Opium, she took opium," Bongnyeo said, trying to suppress her anger.

Opium… Soonboon had doubted Kumok's behavior in the past, but never thought that she had been using opium. She thought the use of the drug was just a story from some other girls. She was worried about the yellowish sap sticking to Kumok's hand, but she wanted to trust her. Until yesterday, really until yesterday, she thought they could escape from here, all three of them.

Whether they succeeded or not, she believed that they could run away if they were all together.

"Kumok can't go with us. No, she can't," Bongnyeo said stiffly, laying Kumok back down on the floor.

"No, we have to leave together," Soonboon whispered.

"No, she can't go like this."

"Wake her up, wake her up and we'll take her," Soonboon nagged.

"It's okay, I will stay here like this. I like it here, just like this. I want to sleep more, don't worry about me, and leave, both of you," Kumok said in her sleep. Her words were unclear and her pronunciation inarticulate.

"What the hell are you talking about? I can't go without you. Please, get real."

Soonboon held her shoulders and shook them.

"I am fine, you girls go. You should leave, go back to your hometowns."

Kumok tried to smile, but she couldn't.

"Get up, hurry. I brought some breakfast, have some. Please, get focused."

Soonboon tried to stand Kumok up, but she fell down like deflated dough.

"It is useless," Bongnyeo said stiffly next to her.

"I can't leave without taking Kumok," Soonboon's voice was choked with tears.

"Go, follow her. I am fine," Kumok said, her eyes barely open. Bongnyeo looked at Kumok for a while then stood up silently.

"Where are you going?"

Bongnyeo didn't answer her and left Kumok's room without saying anything.

"Follow her," Kumok told Soonboon, and Soonboon looked back and forth between her face and Bongnyeo's back.

"Go, hurry," Kumok urged her to follow Bongnyeo.

"How about you?"

"I am okay, go with her."

Soonboon's eyes kept alternating between Kumok and Bongnyeo's back.

"You girls go and escape from this hell. I am fine. You will have a tough time if I go with you, so run away as soon as you can," her words were mumbled and unclear.

"Sorry, I am so sorry," Soonboon told and hugged her tightly.

"You should make it without me..." Kumok said with a faint smile.

But soon, her eyes got wet, and the white parts of her eyes turned red.

"I am okay. Sure, I am fine," she muttered as if talking in her sleep. Soonboon let her lie down on the floor and followed Bongnyeo quickly.

"Bongnyeo, Bongnyeo," Soonboon called after her hurriedly.

Bongnyeo had already reached the barbed wire that connected to the mountain slope, avoiding the guard's eyes. The barbed wire thorns looked especially sharp today, but she climbed on the fence and passed over it without a problem. The tall weeds absorbed the noises she made. As she hid under the shadow of the forest, a guard looked at the spot where Bongnyeo had just jumped from. The shadow of the lonely forest covered Bongnyeo cunningly.

There was less surveillance since the mountain had rough, irregular sides. The unfathomable, dark, remote slope was a natural fortress and an obstacle. Soonboon was surprised at Bongnyeo's speed. Even though she had prepared to escape, she never thought Bongnyeo could pass over the wire so quickly. I should bring the bag of cookies the girl gave me, Soonboon remembered, but she had to follow Bongnyeo now. It was too late to get the cookies, she did not have time to hesitate.

Soonboon feigned indifference and waited until the guard looked elsewhere. When his eyes looked away, she could pass over the barbed wire lightly and secretly like a butterfly, reach Bongnyeo and hide with her there. Her mind was busy as she looked over the surroundings.

Fortunately, the surveillance was not as tight as usual during meal time. A soldier walked back and forth around the comfort station, but he seemed tired. He looked around here and there, holding a gun on his shoulder, but his mind seemed far away. Bongnyeo urged Soonboon with her eyes from her safe, shadowy hiding spot. "Come here, hurry up," she beckoned with her eyes. Soonboon was parched with thirst. She couldn't even swallow her dry saliva, worried about making any noise. She waited for the right time, and kept looking sideways at the barbed wire wall she would have to pass.

It was Soonboon's turn; she should pass over the barbed wire as soon as possible. *My turn, right, it's my turn.* Soonboon's heart pounded with extreme tension. Her hands were wet with sweat, and her pounding heart was out of control. She tried to relieve her anxiety with deep breaths, but her heart beat even more, she had to go now, to pass over the wall that seemed like a border between this life and the next.

"Hurry up," she felt like Bongnyeo was telling her. Hurry, it's time. Jump over now, quickly. Soonboon lowered her posture and prepared to jump as the guard's eyes turned to another place. Her posture was agile, like a cat's.

In the meantime, the morning sunshine was getting hotter and hotter with each passing moment. But Soonboon couldn't even move one step forward because of her excessive anxiety. Bongnyeo stuck her head out and hid under the shadow, heavy with worries about Soonboon missing her chance every time. Soon, Bongnyeo's sunlit face clearly showed impatience and blame. She should do it anyhow. She had to jump over to survive and have a dream again for a future.

Soonboon let out a deep breath again, she should not hesitate anymore. They should run as far as possible before meal time ended. Well, it's now or never, hurry! Soonboon felt Bongnyeo's eyesight from across the clumps of grass. The guard's eyes passed by the wall that Soonboon should jump over, and looked elsewhere. Right now! Soonboon ran to the barbed wire like she was attracted to it, and grabbed it. She didn't care that her clothes stuck to the wire thorns. Everybody could have a super power in an extremely dangerous moment. Soonboon jumped over the wire finally. The height was taller than she thought. When she jumped down from the wall, a dull shock came from her soles and traveled up her whole body, but she couldn't scream. The grass absorbed the sound like it had for Bongnyeo, but the vibration spread out in all directions in the morning air. The morning sun flooded the earth intensely.

Soonboon hid her body close to Bongnyeo. The guard's eyes scanned past their hiding spot, but he could see only the sun. The sunlight was passive and nonchalant like nothing had happened, like the previous sound was an audible hallucination. The guard stared at that spot for a long time. He stuck his head out in the direction of the sound, his head twisting this way and that way.

Soonboon and Bongnyeo squeezed their bodies into a tree to hide from the guard's eyes, and didn't breathe. Their hearts were pounding loudly that they could hear their own heartbeats in their ears. They didn't just listen to their own heartbeats, but each other's. Their mouths watered, but they couldn't swallow, in case it made a sound. Soonboon held Bongnyeo's hand. Bongnyeo's palm was wet with nerveousness. She always looked strong but perhaps she was scared at this moment. Soonboon held her hand tightly again, and Bongnyeo also gripped back; the power of their grasp was so powerful. They depended on each other now.

When the guard's expression finally looked uninterested and turned his back to look in another direction, they went toward the mountain. They didn't know what they would meet after passing it. However, they had to move far away from this place. Then, whatever was next would be next. To escape from this hell was the only thing they decided to think about now.

It was not easy to pass over the wooded hill. Overgrown thorn bushes were here and there, and the thorns scratched and poked their flesh when they passed. When the sharp thorns scratched them, blood seeped out from the skin. But their nervousness, fear, and impatience overwhelmed the pain. Their knees knocked together, and they were afraid someone would suddenly appear and grab their necks, or the icy muzzle of a gun would aim at the backs of their heads. Soonboon and Bongnyeo were quiet. They needed to walk another step instead of talking. Getting farther away from the compound alive was their only goal; they had to walk as fast as possible to do that.

Just then, the siren sounds rang sharply. It was different from the sound of the air-raid alert. Soonboon and Bongnyeo knew the meaning of the siren. They must have noticed that two girls had disappeared. Their hearts pounded fiercely as if they would burst into pieces. The girls ran forward neck and neck. They couldn't stop even if they slipped and fell. They knew they would die if they stopped, so they had to run desperately. The siren kept ringing with consecutive short breaks. The remained girls might be held under the thrashing whip, or might not be free from the strict surveillance. *What is Kumok doing?* Soonboon kept remembering Kumok's hollow eyes and her tears.

"I should have brought Kumok," Soonboon said as she panted. But no answer came from Bongnyeo ahead; only her irregular breathing was heard. The siren kept ringing as they ran.

29. Being Arrested

They walked and walked frantically. They didn't stop no matter how much they slipped and fell. No, they couldn't. They heard barking from far away, *ruff, ruff, ruff...*

"Ouch!"

Just ahead Bongnyeo fell down with a short scream. She must have not seen a tough vine near the rock. She grimaced and groaned, holding her leg.

"Are you all right?" Soonboon asked, her face soaked with sweat. But Bongnyeo let out a groan instead of answering. No, she tried to tolerate the pain, but accidentally groaned as she breathed out.

"Can you walk?"

Bongnyeo tried to stand up, but they just realized that her left leg was broken. The barking sound was getting closer.

"I can't go. You'd better go without me."

Bongnyeo pushed Soonboon away with a wrinkled face.

"No. I can't go without you."

"Go, please go."

"No, I can't."

"Why are you acting like this all the time? Go by yourself!"

"Try to walk, slowly."

"No, you go by yourself, go, please!"

Bongnyeo's face was distorted with pain.

"Please leave fast, I will take care of everything from now on, go!"

"Hold my hands."

"No, I can't, please go by yourself."

"Hold my hands."

Bongnyeo held Soonboon's hand as if she couldn't help it due to Soonboon's constant insistence. Soonboon kept going forward step by step while holding Bongnyeo's hand tightly.

"No, I can't. I can't go anymore in this condition. I'd better sit down."

Soonboon went down the hill since Bongnyeo couldn't get through the thorn bushes and steep road with her broken leg. She hopped on one foot, limped sometimes, and sat down as if she couldn't stand it anymore. Every time, Soonboon helped Bongnyeo stand up and walk.

When they had barely come down from the mountain, they saw the gate of the military station. Although they ran away as if escaping to death, they had only reached the front of the gate. Soonboon felt all her energy drain away suddenly. Bongnyeo hardened her face as if she was disappointed as well. There was no place to hide. The crooked road looked like a snake; there were neither houses nor people.

The sun was already over their heads, blazing over them. If there was a slight splash of rain, it might cool off. But the road might be muddied by the rain which would make it hard to walk. They were thirsty, they felt like their tongues had turned to wood from their thirst.

"Please go by yourself, please."

Bongnyeo urged again, pushing Soonboon away.

"No way, we will die together or live together. How can I go by myself and leave you here like this? No, I can't. I can't go without you, please go with me."

Soonboon's tone was more resolute than usual.

"Why are you so stubborn?"

Bongnyeo was angry at her, but Soonboon didn't care.

"Hurry, let's go. If you are worried about me, just walk slowly."

Soonboon encouraged and urged her, but Soonboon knew they couldn't go farther with her in this condition.

Just then: "There you are, you ungrateful bitches."

Three soldiers appeared abruptly in front of them and blocked the two girls, aiming their guns at them. They hadn't seen any soldiers just a few moments ago, where had they come from? The dogs next to them growled, showing their white teeth as if they were about to attack the girls. Thick saliva ran down their teeth, the ropes tied to their necks tense as though they would break soon. The dogs lifted their front legs and growled like they were ready to bite them if the ropes were untied.

"How dare you bitches run away?"

One slanty-eyed soldier grabbed Soonboon's hair. She was forced to let go of Bongnyeo's arms, and she dropped down on the ground letting out a short scream.

"You are out of your minds, we all treated you so nicely. Fine, then I will make you realize the truth."

Soonboon tried with all her strength to escape from the hands gripping her hair. Whenever she tried more, the grip on her hair got stronger.

"The Japanese Emperor in this wartime gave you food and clothes and let you live in luxury, yet you tried to run away? What ingratitude, bitches. Okay. I will show you today what your reward is for this."

Soonboon begged the soldier gripping her. "Please let me go, please..." The other soldier kicked Bongnyeo's shin with his military boots where she was sitting on the floor. Bongnyeo screamed and fell down on her side.

"Was it you? Did you instigate her?"

It was a signal and a beginning. Two soldiers attacked Bongnyeo and stamped down on her mercilessly with their heavy boots and muskets. Bongnyeo buried her head in her arms as they kicked and struck her.

"Stop, stop it," Soonboon shouted to the two soldiers as they kicked and stamped on Bongnyeo.

"You crazy bitch, how dare you yell at us? Fine, are you worried about your friend? Let's see how much you care about your friend. Do you want to die instead of this bitch? Are you going to die to save this bitch?"

The soldier who grabbed Soonboon's hair released her and aimed his gun at her. The muzzle of the weapon was pointed at Soonboon's heart.

"Answer, do you want to die or do you want me to kill your friend?"

Soonboon couldn't breathe. The muzzle of the gun looked like the eye of a beast, that blackish hole, the hole that was staring at her life without shaking. Everything will end when the black hole blasts. She might take her last breath without knowing it was about to explode. The two soldiers stopped kicking Bongnyeo, and looked at Soonboon. They looked at her with strange smiles on their faces.

"Answer, you or your friend?"

Soonboon folded her hands, then begged.

"Please save us, we were wrong."

"I am asking again. You or your friend?"

"Please save us, please…"

Soonboon approached Bongnyeo and hugged her. Bongnyeo's face was distorted with misery. The muzzle of the gun followed her. This time, the gun muzzle aimed at the two girls, both.

"I will kill both of you if you don't answer. Answer! Who do you want to die? Anyone who answers first will survive."

"Kill me, sons of bitches!" Bongnyeo answered.

The blackish gun muzzle now turned toward Bongnyeo. Soonboon shouted and blocked her from the gun.

"Please save her. Please don't kill her."

"Move away!"

They struck Soonboon's chest with the gun's nose. She felt like she would urinate because of the firm and cold feeling of the gun. Death was right under her nose. It could fire away, and she could be dead within seconds. Or rather, she would become a ghost in the afterlife. However, she couldn't allow Bongnyeo to stand in front of the muzzle of the gun. She couldn't push Bongnyeo toward them to save herself.

"I will count to three. One! Two! Three!"

"Shoot me."

Bongnyeo shouted while pushing Soonboon away, and now the gun aimed at Bongnyeo again.

"Aha, fine, I will kill you, but not in here, I will kill you in front of all the other bitches."

"No, please save us," Soonboon begged again, rubbing her palms together.

"Take them."

With a terse command, Bongnyeo was thrown into the truck bed like a package. Soonboon followed Bongnyeo, then hugged her.

"Tell them to save you, beg them to save yourself."

But Bongnyeo remained silent.

•   •   •

30. Back to the Comfort Station

The truck drove the two girls back into the comfort station. Bongnyeo remained calm as if she had given everything up. Her calmness weighed heavily on Soonboon like a sore sorrow. But what more could she expect? The passing scenery and the bright sun on her head didn't give her any joy. It seemed like a landscape in a picture or a world that existed far away from her that was not related to her. The military station encircled with barbed wire looked the same as usual. The guards with guns on their shoulders walked around the station normally, and the comfort station was surrounded by horrendous gloom. Soonboon felt all her blood run backward in her veins seeing the station again. Like thorns were in her blood cells, she felt like them poke inside her body and attack her. She sensed her legs numbing and her body stiffening. Bongnyeo had a placid expression at that moment.

"Get down!"

The butt of the musket struck Soonboon's shoulder as the words were spoken. Soonboon felt a deep pain as if her shoulder was broken from the gun that flew into her without giving her a chance to avoid it. Soonboon assisted Bongnyeo, but it was difficult for her to stand up right away. Her broken leg was already swollen. Bongnyeo groaned in spite of herself as she took a step forward.

"Why don't you get down, lazy bitches?"

The soldiers cursed at them impatiently. Bongnyeo screamed as they dragged her down to the floor. Her broken leg was forced to step on the ground, but they didn't care.

Kanemura, with the nickname of the grim reaper, came out upon hearing Bongnyeo's scream. The soldiers who had caught Bongnyeo and Soonboon saluted him. His upper body shook in a mannerly salute.

"I caught the runaway bitches."

He skimmed Bongnyeo and Soonboon with small eyes, full of a horrifying sparkle.

"Did you think you could run away? How dare you reward the Japanese Emperor like this, when he gave you meals and clothes? Ungrateful bitches! I will make you regret to the core the stupid things you did!" Kanemura grabbed Soonboon's hair when he finished talking. Her mind was completely blank as he roughly grabbed her hair all at once. She felt like her neck was broken.

"You will appreciate this moment later," he whispered into her ear through clenched teeth. Kanemura's humid breath lingered on her ear lobe, making her shudder.

"Tie them on the pillar. They will be an example. I will convict them in front of all the girls."

Right after these words fell, the soldier took Soonboon and Bongnyeo to the front of the comfort station, set the pillar next to the guard post, and tied them to it. He checked the knot over and over in case it might untie, pulling on the rope again to make sure. But the rope, round and tight, didn't move at all. Their skin began to sting and become numb where the rope touched them. Soonboon was thirsty, she felt like sand was in her mouth, but she couldn't drink at all. The comfort station seemed as if it shook in a haze of heat. The long line of soldiers at each girl's room looked like an illusion.

The girls' bodies were wearing down from satisfying the smelly soldiers' bestial desires constantly. Their bodies were wet with soldiers' saliva and bodily fluids, and many were on the bridge of collapse. On early spring days, fallen magnolia leaves would crumble to brown; similarly, the girls were crumbling from diseases, ready to blow away, disintegrate, disappear from the world.

In the meantime, the golden and bluish color of evening dusk visited them. The shadow that had started at their feet was getting longer. It looked like a bizarre clump that was stretching its height but would disappear as night approached gently. The darkness progressed to a pitch-black night, and its thickness wiped out the world.

Soonboon felt no pain as if she were made of wood, all her senses having disappeared as the circulation was cut off from her arms.

"Are you okay?" Soonboon asked softly, but Bongnyeo remained quiet.

"Are you sleeping? How is your leg?"

Still, no response came. No, there were sounds; there existed the sounds of night insects that came out now after avoiding the extreme noon heat, and the echoes of guard's footsteps ricocheting. All other sounds were absorbed in the darkness, and a strange silence started to sink in. Bongnyeo wasn't moving at all, and her inaction weighed on Soonboon a lot. It was not easy to stay still in the same position with a broken leg. She could twist her body or let out a groan, but she remained strangely quiet and immobile. Soonboon asked Bongnyeo again and waited for her answer.

"Bongnyeo, let's go home, let's go back alive. You wanted to go to school. You can make it. We can't die here like this, we can't, we have to go home alive. You can study, then I…"

'Will get married,' she wanted to say, but she stopped there. *I am too far from getting married, can I even go back home? Can I go back to the straw-covered house that lies down like an animal? How can I see mom, dad, my friends, and neighbors, while pretending like nothing happened?*

"Bongnyeo, you have to study, you are smart. You can make it though others can't, so please hang on a little bit more."

Soonboon comforted Bongnyeo with a firm voice, but she didn't respond. She only changed her posture as if feeling pain in her leg. This movement soothed Soonboon, it meant she was still alive.

Butterfly, where are you? Soonboon wondered. If only the butterfly could fly to her right now… but sleep came over her instead. Sleep occupied her consciousness even in this horrific situation, as she was firmly tied, standing up. Yet sleeping helped her to forget what was happening.

"Soonboon, it's me, wake up."

Soonboon was disturbed by some strange sound calling her in the darkness. *Is it my butterfly?* Soonboon tried to catch the sound, opening her eyes slightly.

"Drink this. Hurry, before somebody sees."

Kumok brought a bowl of water to Soonboon's mouth.

"Drink."

Kumok hurried her and looked around. Soonboon drank the water, and it poured past her mouth. She was sorry for wasting the water. As some flowed down her throat, she felt her spirits waking up.

"How about Bongnyeo? Can you give some to Bongnyeo as well?"

"She already had some."

Soonboon felt something stuck in her solar plexus, but she felt real relief at Kumok's saying that Bongnyeo drank some water.

"I wished you had made it out when you ran away. Far, far away where they couldn't find you."

Soonboon didn't say anything back.

"The other girls were disappointed even if they didn't mention it."

Soonboon would have made it. She wished she could have run far away and told the world about this brutality and cruelty. *No, no,* she thought. These were nightmares and memories that should be buried deeply. If the truth was released to the world, the girls might be in bigger trouble than if they said nothing.

"It must hurt." Kumok was sorry for Bongnyeo's swollen broken leg.

"Go back to your room. You will be in trouble if they notice you here."

Soonboon tried to send Kumok back to her room.

Just then, the guard walking around the military station stood and looked down at them. Soonboon and Kumok stopped moving and were quiet as death. But he whistled shortly right after that, and the lights at military station turned on.

"Go, hurry, I don't want you in trouble."

Soonboon rushed Kumok. She stepped backward slowly and ran to the comfort station following Soonboon's words.

"What's up?"

A soldier came to the girls, his face annoying. Fortunately, Kumok was already hiding back in the comfort station. The soldier noticed a dropped bowl next to Soonboon and kicked it. He didn't make any more fuss. He seemed very sleepy and bothered, and he just checked that the rope was tied well, and went back to his position.

31. The Choice

Morning came again without fail and the sun was shining as usual. But this time Soonboon acknowledged that she had no hope to escape from this hell. She didn't know what would happen to them today, but something from yesterday's escape attempt made her calm. Then she realized her body was still tied to a pole outside the barrack. Her nervousness and fear expanded, not knowing what was waiting for her and Bongnyeo that day.

"Bongnyeo," Soonboon fearfully called out to Bongnyeo.

"Don't be afraid," Bongnyeo answered in a hoarse voice.

She seemed afraid as well, considering she responded right away after the long hours of silence last night.

"Are they going to kill us? They must. Right? They will kill us."

Soonboon's heart beat rapidly.

"It's fine if they kill us. It is meaningless to live here like this," Bongnyeo answered in a hideously calm voice, which broke Soonboon's heart.

She felt girls turning their eyes to look at her as they busily prepared for the day. They had to clean their rooms, wash their faces and prepare to start the day before breakfast distribution. They would probably continue with this routine until they died.

The girls' faces were highlighted with the sunshine as they looked at her. She was in the same shoes as she was a few days ago, before this whole event happened.

Her heart saddened looking at the girls who were on the border of life and death in the comfort station, but she knew she was about to turn into a main character of this tragedy now.

Just then, a soldier approached the comfort station and forced the girls toward Bongnyeo and Soonboon by whistling. The girls poured out from all around, forced by the whistle.

"Move quickly," he yelled and the girls came out in droves. They sat down in front of the two girls, following orders.

"I will show you all, clearly, what will happen if you run away. This should be your home and the place where you will die. The Imperial Japanese Army fought to the death against the enemy. How dare you run away to save only yourself, when it is your duty to comfort them? This is an ungrateful attitude toward the Great Emperor, it means you deserted the Great Japan and betrayed the remaining girls. Therefore, don't feel any sympathy for them. These bitches betrayed you. Look at them closely. Watch carefully what will happen today."

He threatened the girls under the bright sky. Dazzling sun rays drifted right in front of Soonboon's face, and it became too bright to open her eyes.

"Bring it here."

He ordered a man with his chin. Following his order, two soldiers brought forward a wooden board and put it on the ground near two girls. What were they going to do? It looked like the bottom lining of a coffin, had nails all over it, but the sharp parts were pointed towards the sky. The sharp end of the nails glistened under the sun. The soldier's lips twisted oddly into a wicked smile. He looked dirty, nasty, cruel.

"These self-centered bitches, betrayers. I will make them wake up to their fullest."

All the girls looked at the board of nails. What is he going to do with it? They were all asking each other in silence with curious expressions.

"Untie them."

He ordered his subordinates to untie the rope. His voice sounded solemn, like that of a chief priest.

"You can survive if you obey me, but you shall die if you don't."

All the girls remained silent. Soonboon's heart stomped.

Soonboon and Bongnyeo were dragged in front of the wooden board and stood side by side. He walked around the two girls with his hands on his back. He cleared his throat a couple of times and said nothing for a while. Only his evil eyes shone under the shadow of the rim of his hat. His silence increased the girls' fear and tension.

"Okay."

Just then, he stood up and looked at Soonboon and then at Bongnyeo. "You first!"

He pointed at Bongnyeo. Soonboon felt her throat lock up at that moment. She was glad that he didn't point at her, not right now, not right now. But she should not be happy for that. He didn't speak for a while after pointing at Bongnyeo. He just looked at her face, but he only noticed that she was calm. She was quiet as if saying that she was ready to die if he touched her. He was betrayed by Bongnyeo's calmness, and his eyes grew fiercer.

"Roll over it!"

Ahaaa... the girls groaned, shocked at his words, but Bongnyeo looked down the nail board with a stolid expression. The sun shone coldly, reflecting off the ends of the nails; their points looked sharper in the shocking light.

"Roll over the board. You will survive if you roll over it. Otherwise, you shall die."

However, Bongnyeo stood like a statue with a hard look.

"I repeat, roll over it!"

He forced her again with a loud voice, but she didn't move at all. The girls were intensely anxious as they looked at her.

"This bitch hasn't obeyed me yet. Okay, fine. I highly compliment your upright spirit, but I will continue until you can't resist."

His voice softened a little bit, and he retained a greasy smile as he glared at Bongnyeo's eyes, and he approached Soonboon.

"Hmmm."

Soonboon was horrified, and she nearly peed. He looked at Soonboon and took out the parade sword from the sheath on his waist. The sound of metal friction gave her goosebumps. The sword divided the air as the wind blew. It happened in a moment. Soonboon closed her eyes. She almost peed when she reopened her eyes. I'm not dead. She felt that her neck was cut, but she was still breathing.

"If you keep resisting, this bitch will die. Do you want to roll over it or do you want me to kill her?" he said to Bongnyeo with a sly smile. His eyes glittered murderously. A groan spread out again among the girls. He looked at them as they groaned, and then looked back to Bongnyeo again.

"You choose. As an officer of Great Japan who has received grace from the Great Emperor, I will respect your choice in place of him."

However, Bongnyeo didn't move willingly. Soonboon's heart pounded outside of her chest. This morning was too cruel to her, too painful, too sad and too much... She wished she could die rather than live like an animal but would she still rather live than die? He asked again impatiently as Bongnyeo still did not move:

"This bitch or you?"

"Bongnyeo," Soonboon called her name in spite of herself. Soonboon didn't understand herself why she called Bongnyeo, or what she wanted from her. She didn't know whether she would let her die or save her.

"Bongnyeo! Bongnyeo!" Soonboon called repeatedly, like a chorus. Bongnyeo looked back at her as she called out, her face stiff.

"I will count until three, want to roll on it or kill her?"

The girls didn't groan at all now, and just watched the three standing before them. Only the morning sun chatted with the sky.

"One!"

Soonboon stopped breathing.

"Two!"

It seemed his voice froze the sun.

"Three!"

Soonboon closed her eyes. *I will die.*

Just then, a scream burst out among the girls. Soonboon opened her eyes, surprised by the scream. Bongnyeo had begun to roll over the wooden board in a flash. She rolled on the board driven densely with nails. The girls' sharp screaming split the air and seemed to rip up the sky, some girls shut their eyes and lowered their heads so as not to watch it anymore. Bongnyeo's clothes were torn in an instant and soaked with blood, but she never screamed at all. Her flesh was torn and opened in different parts, yet she never groaned with pain. Pieces of her flesh and clothes stayed on the nails. Soonboon felt like her own flesh was being torn. No, not even her flesh: her heart, the sky and everything was being torn into pieces. Bongnyeo never screamed at all until the end. She just rolled over the board of nails, her mouth shut and her eyes tightly closed.

The soldier's face was distorted as he watched her. He approached her, shutting his mouth and putting his hands on his back as she finished rolling over the board. Bongnyeo couldn't help her face from falling apart with pain. Her body was covered with blood mixed with flesh and pieces of ripped cloth, making it hard to distinguish what was what. The girls wished it would be over soon as they moaned and cried. Soonboon couldn't say any words. She might have rolled if Bongnyeo hadn't. It might be her turn next, so her whole body was numb with fear.

"Roll over it again."

He spoke slowly. The girls looked at each other in disbelief.

"Why are you hesitating? I said roll over it again." His voice trembled slightly with anger. He took out his sword again and struck Bongnyeo's back with the back of it, making her fall to the ground.

"Roll over it again." His voice was nervous this time.

The girls watched Bongnyeo, their mouths open with fear, but she was as steady as a rock. Then the officer approached Soonboon and brought the sword to her neck. He shouted to Bongnyeo as he stared at her:

"Do you want to roll over it or do you want me to kill her?" Slowly, Bongnyeo started to roll on the board again. Soonboon peed at last...

32. Disappeared Bongnyeo

Bongnyeo couldn't walk by herself. She left carried by a handcart. They didn't know whether she was alive or not.

"Did you bitches see that? The same punishment will be given to you if you run away. Nobody can escape from here. You must live here altogether or die with us. You will never die if you obey me accordingly. I don't want you to do anything stupid, understand?"

The girls were too scared to answer. He smiled, satisfied by their faces frozen with fear.

"Go back to your rooms. Do your best to serve the Japanese Imperial Army, even better than previously. Compliment their efforts. If you don't listen, you will never have any forgiveness or generosity, you will be punished. Got it?"

But the girls remained quiet, petrified, and they just looked at him.

"Why don't you answer, bitches? Are you out of your minds? Do you want me to make you get real?" Just then, some answers scattered out.

"Go back to your places. I will be watching you. Got it?"

"Yes," they answered hesitantly.

Soonboon was forgiven because of the sacrifice of Bongnyeo. She had saved Soonboon. Soonboon went back to her room, mingled in with the other girls. What had happened just now? She couldn't believe it even if she had watched it. *Had I actually been running away? Was it real? Wasn't it a dream? What about Bongnyeo? Where is she? Is she safe, and alive?* Uncertainty filled her head and disappeared in an instant. When she tried to send a signal to Bongnyeo, a soldier came into her room.

"How dare this bitch run away?"

He entered her room roughly, took off her clothes by force and tried to violate her. Soonboon blocked him by strengthening her legs, but he noticed her resisting and slapped her face with his fist. Her lips cracked and bled. He defiled in every way. He smashed and trampled her body, and fulfilled his bestial desire with no regard to the young lady in front of him. Even as she was feeling terrible, piercing sadness.

Right after he went out, another soldier came into her room. He was the friendly Korean from before. He looked at her cracked lips and sat down next to her quietly, as her nosebleed turned into a blood clot.

"I wished you had made it when you ran away."

Soonboon broke into tears at what he said.

"You never listened to me when I asked you to escape with me." His voice sounded a little bit angry at her.

Yes, he surely had asked that. He wanted her to run away since he had first visited her, but she couldn't escape without taking Kumok and Bongnyeo. She didn't want to run away with him by herself, leaving them here in the comfort station. Morning sunshine cut the world into pieces through the curtain in her room. The Korean soldier's clothes looked more ragged now. The sweat smell was horrible and the mud stuck on his military uniform had dried like scales.

He said one day that the forced drafted Koreans would be deployed to the front line, and that they would die at any time. He didn't see some familiar faces anymore, and he knew he could die at any time like them.

"It's not too late even now, please, let's escape this place."

Soonboon listened to what he said in silence.

"Let's run away. If I could die honorably, I would not regret dying here right now, but that's not how it is. Who is this war for? It is for them. Why should we die for them in this war? Please escape with me, and let's live together. Let's go to a place where nobody knows us."

Soonboon shook her head gently at his words and looked at him with eyes full of tears.

"Please run away with me."

"Didn't you see what I experienced just now? We can't make it."

"You just follow me."

"Do you know where we are? How can I escape when I don't know where I am? There's no place to hide even if we run away."

"Isn't it better than dying here in vain?"

"No, I can't, no, I don't want to."

Soonboon shook her head strongly this time. She was afraid and horrified even thinking about it. She never wanted to encounter that again. It would be better to die here even in vain, no, she hated all men anyhow.

"Don't say no so easily, please consider it again."

He held her arms and shook them, begging her. But Soonboon's head was whirling with thoughts of Bongnyeo. What had happened to her? Was she alive or not? Nobody had said anything about Bongnyeo.

33. Bongnyeo's Missing

Bongnyeo's room was empty even at midnight. No sound came from her room. *Knock, knock*. Soonboon knocked on her room several times, but no response ever came.

"Bongnyeo! Bongnyeo!"

She called Bongnyeo in a whisper. She called her name over and over again, but she could only confirm that the darkness was alone in her room.

Knock, knock. Just then, the wall was shaken. It was a signal, but it came from Kumok's room, not Bongnyeo's. Soonboon crept into her room.

"What happened to Bongnyeo? Have you heard about her?"

Soonboon asked about Bongnyeo as soon as she saw Kumok. She thought someone who had visited Kumok's room might have said something.

"I don't know," Kumok shook her head.

But somehow Kumok seemed weak, powerless as if she was melted chocolate in the summer. Soonboon asked again argumentatively, "Did you, did you have opium?"

"No!" Kumok denied, surprised at Soonboon's question, but she still looked conspicuous.

"Come here." Soonboon pulled Kumok toward her, but Kumok pushed away her hands and turned her head aside.

"Tell me honestly, did you have any opium?"

"I said no," Kumok repeated, seeming less confident this time. Soonboon asked while holding Kumok's arms, "What are you going to do? You, silly girl. Didn't you see what happened to the other girls who used opium?"

"I know."

"How could you take it if you knew?"

"I don't."

"Don't lie to me." Kumok didn't deny it anymore since Soonboon kept asking.

"You can't quit once you're addicted, you'll be hooked. Do you want to be a junkie? Do you want to die here in vain? Do you really want that?"

"Can we go back home?" Kumok asked while staring at a dark spot as Soonboon scolded her.

"So? Did you have opium? Sure, we can go home, why couldn't we?"

"In this condition? With this body? What are you going to do there? Can we go back to live like we did before we came here? Do you really think it is possible?"

Soonboon couldn't answer this time. She would like to say 'we can make it' through her mouth, but she couldn't. *Indeed, can I go back home with this body, like Kumok said? Can I go back and see my parents pretending nothing happened?*

"No, I can't go. I couldn't go even if it was allowed… I'll die here… I can't stand a moment without opium. I can't," Kumok cried.

They didn't say anything more for a while after that. Strange, anonymous sounds came from someone's room. A soldier was violating a girl. They didn't know exactly where the sound came from. The sound lowered and echoed in the night, and the echo prevented them from guessing the origin of the sound.

"Foolish little bitch, stupid slut," she overheard. Soonboon was not sure who the soldier was cursing at. The unknown soldier kept saying "stupid bitch" as he violated the girl.

"Where is Bongnyeo?" Soonboon asked, but Kumok didn't respond.

"Is she alive or not?"

"She might be dead. She was barely alive… She would come back to her room if she were alive," Kumok said without looking at Soonboon.

"She could be alive, I think. She is stronger than others. She is different from us."

"But…" Kumok didn't finish her words, she was not sure. *Thump! Thump!* Someone was coming up the stairs.

"Go back to your room, someone is coming. It might be Kanemura."

Kumok rushed Soonboon back out to her room. Unsurprisingly, a man's voice came from Kumok's room, and it was Kanemura. He visited Kumok that evening and went back out at dawn.

34. Bongnyeo

Ring, ring. The bell clang to notify the start of the day. Soonboon felt a pain as if her body was squeezing itself before relaxing again. Her body remembered what had happened yesterday, and reminded her of the pain.

Soonboon went to the well to do laundry. The morning sun spread lazily around the military station as usual. The sun was cunning this morning. She looked around the place, everybody was walking around, yawning with bloated faces. The soldier who completed his shift went back to the barrack with sleepy eyes. The girls cleaned outside of their rooms, went to the well to wash clothes with Soonboon, or went to the meal distribution station for breakfast. However, Bongnyeo was nowhere to be seen. "Where the hell is Bongnyeo?" Soonboon asked the girls she met. "Have you heard anything about Bongnyeo?" Everybody shook their heads. 'Have you heard about Bongnyeo?' She asked with her eyes, but the answer was the same, no. Soonboon put the laundry in the wash tub and fetched water, but her brain was entirely occupied with thoughts of Bongnyeo.

Just then, a loud siren sounded. It was an air raid siren. Soonboon hurried out from the well and hid under a tree. Lots of alerts had gone off recently. The tide of war seemed unusual considering the frequency of sirens occurred increasing. The soldiers also seemed even more tired. A tension flowed through the military station. Soonboon didn't understand why they had this war they called holy- a time of killing and being killed. If they died during the war, what did their death mean?

"Go back to your original spot. Keep doing your work."

The warning was cleared, and a soldier rushed the girls out. It seemed like they were spared, or the warning could have been wrong. Soldiers became more violent after coming back from intense battles, when preparing for one or if the air raid warning went off. They were powerless about the present, not knowing when they would die, so they became obsessed with the girls' bodies because of their impending death.

Soonboon grabbed the laundry again as she left the shadow of the forest. She did the laundry halfheartedly. Her mind and thoughts were filled with musings on Bongnyeo's safety and whereabouts. *Ring, ring.* As soon as she finished the laundry, the bell tolled to notify them of meal distribution. *Ring, ring.* The bell after a warning siren sounded softer. The girls gathered around the station as the bell rang, but Bongnyeo was still nowhere to be seen.

The meal looked different than usual. They generally served a rice ball with pickled radish, sometimes only the rice ball, but there was a big iron pot today. Hot vapor rose from it.

"Okay. You will have a special meal today. I compliment all your efforts to comfort the Imperial Japanese Army. The armies are ready to die for their country and want to die for it. This is all thanks to your efforts and loyalty. They might miss their hometown and family, but they can stand it thanks to your effort, so I praise your work. While the brave Imperial Japanese Army is winning the battle every day, you do a great job as well. Therefore, I have prepared a special meal as a reward for you."

The badge on his shoulder glittered under the sun. Whenever he talked, his shoulders moved up and down, and his badge seemed to pop up each time.

"Now, form a line and receive the meal one by one."

As soon as his words stopped, the girls were curious about what it would be.

"What is it? What is the special meal?"

"Smells different. It's a warm soup."

"They are trying to comfort us since the girls tried to run away, they want to prevent us from running away in the future."

The girls put on happy faces and seemed to already feel full as they looked at the rising hot vapors. *Is this true? Is this really true? Is this a special meal to console the girls?* Soonboon was not sure.

"Come this way." Kumok pulled on Soonboon's hand and let her stand in front.

"It's unusual. A special meal, what is it?" Kumok whispered in her ear.

"How about Bongnyeo? Have you heard about Bongnyeo?"

"Well, she might be somewhere since she was hurt a lot that day," Kumok answered her glumly. Meanwhile, Soonboon's eyes couldn't stay in one place. She only thought about where Bongnyeo might be.

Finally, Soonboon's turn had come. The man who had forced Bongnyeo roll over the nail board threatened Soonboon, standing next to the soldier who served the steaming hot soup.

"Is that you who was caught running away? How dare you run away? Okay. You are so brave. But, remember, your life is worthless than that of a fly, so stay as still as a dead mouse if you wish to survive. You got it?"

The serving of hot meat soup this morning was unusual. Rainbow-colored oil floated on top. It was the first time they had meat soup since she arrived the comfort station. The officers ate animals and cattle sometimes, but the girls never had any meat.

"Is it meat soup? What a surprise!" Kumok approached Soonboon while holding her own bowl. She was walking carefully to avoid pouring it on the floor.

"It could be a conciliatory gesture to prevent us from fleeing again, after what they did to Bongnyeo yesterday," Soonboon copied what other girls were saying.

"Maybe they aren't just monsters, since they are trying to console us."

"So what? They do exactly what beasts do."

"That's right. How long has it been since I last had meat soup? But what kind of meat is this? It doesn't seem like beef, is it monkey meat? There are lots of monkeys around here." Kumok said as she stirred it with her spoon.

"Maybe," Soonboon answered.

Soonboon didn't want to eat, overwhelmed with her thoughts of Bongnyeo. How could she eat when she didn't even know whether Bongnyeo was alive or not, after she had sacrificed herself for Soonboon?

"Well, today is a special day, so eat everything and don't leave leftovers, then focus on comforting the Imperial Japanese Army when your energy is up. You shall never run away anymore. I will never forgive you if it happens again." The officer warned as he looked around at the girls. He cooed sometimes and threatened other times.

"Eat it," Kumok said to Soonboon, but she was worried so about Bongnyeo.

Where on earth was she? Soonboon was sorry for holding a bowl of meat soup here by herself. She should have gone with Bongnyeo.

The girls enjoyed the warm soup. Breakfast time was happy, cheerful, and noisy as they ate their first meat soup since arriving the comfort station. Just then, an officer stopped in front of Soonboon after walking around bragging toward the girls enjoying their soup.

"Why don't you eat? Don't you like meat soup?" he glared down at her. Kumok quickly put her spoon in Soonboon's hand, surprised.

"Eat it," he said again. Soonboon took a careful sip.

"Eat all of it. You won't survive if you have any leftovers. It is like committing treason if you don't finish all the precious food provided by the Great Japanese Emperor. So eat all of it. I am so generous that I will give you one more bowl of soup, so eat."

"Eat quickly." Kumok nudged her worriedly after the officer's order. Soonboon was uncomfortable about his sharp eyes watching her. She brought the bowl to her mouth.

She actually missed the toughness of the rice ball. She was almost vomiting because from the burnt taste of oil in her mouth, but she swallowed carefully, worried he would notice her discomfort. She swallowed over and over again. He smiled, satisfied as he watched her eat. His smile was ugly.

"Good, that's good. You should obey just like that. You will die if you don't obey. Understand?" he confirmed again and stood up.

"Eat it, so you can survive. You wanted to go back home. You wanted to get married there, so eat it. If you finish the bowl, he will give you another. Eat more, so you can survive," Kumok said soothingly. Soonboon's stomach was upset, but she said nothing.

He seemed satisfied as he looked at the girls who were enjoying the soup. His face was full of arrogance as if he was providing them with an enormous grace.

"Did you like that? I already had two bowls. It tasted better than I thought."

He continued; "Now, if you finish everything, work harder than you worked before."

But suddenly, he stopped talking for a moment and looked at the girls. A sly smile spread across his face. Then he continued. "You bitches looked as if you liked it. It should be good since it was made with meat."

He stopped speaking again and looked around the girls.

"Do you know what you had just now?"

He stopped talking for a moment again, then smiled as he looked around at each girl's face, one by one. His smile was horrific, then he continued very slowly:

"You ate your friend just now. The meat you had so deliciously was your friend." He was laughing viciously looking at the girls' faces. The girls didn't understand what he said at the beginning. What the hell is he talking about? They looked at each other as if to ask what he meant.

"We made the soup with that bitch, your friend."

The girls doubted if they heard correctly. After looking each other's eyes and his sly smile, they finally figured out what his words meant. Inexpressible emotions crossed their faces: some grimaced and started to retch, holding their stomachs, some girls ran to find water, others vomited on the ground. Soonboon puked out all the food that she had eaten hesitantly. The food hadn't even landed in her stomach when it reflexed back through her esophagus.

"You!"

He pointed out Soonboon.

"Is that you again?"

Kumok was trembling, about to cry with worry for Soonboon beside her.

As he strode forward, he pouted his lips with an ugly expression and the girls' worried faces followed his steps.

"Did you forget what I just said? Eat it."

He said rowdily, looking at Soonboon's puke. The vomit from her esophagus soaked into the earth and solids were scattered on the ground like mush.

"Didn't you hear that? Eat it," he yelled to Soonboon.

The girls gazed at Soonboon with their eyes and held their hands. Eat it, hurry, listen to him, please. Soonboon felt like all her might had drained and she had lost consciousness. I will die. I'd rather die. She shut her eyes to disobey him.

"If you don't obey, you will have only death, but I will teach you how to surrender before I kill you." The back of his sword struck Soonboon's back. She fell on the floor from its force. She felt a pain as if her spine was disconnected and her back, and she couldn't breathe due to the pain. Soonboon didn't scream, but the girls did.

"Eat it. Lick it."

"Soonboon, please eat it, please…"

"I said eat it, bitch!" he ordered her as Kumok begged. Her back ached from the sword's strike.

"Eat it, this is my last warning. If you don't eat it, you will end up just like your friend."

He kicked Soonboon's left side with his clunky boots. The pain twisted around her whole body, stopping her breathing and making her dizzy. Soonboon raised her upper body with one hand holding her side and the other clutching the ground.

Butterfly, butterfly, where are you? Where have all the butterflies gone?

"Soonboon, please…" Kumok begged her as she cried. Soonboon looked at Kumok's distorted mouth, thick saliva flowing through it.

"Soonboon, please obey him, please…"

Kumok looked pitiful. *The girl, the poor young girl, Kumok, what will happen to her if I die?*

Soonboon approached her vomit and brought her tongue toward it. *I am so sorry, Bongnyeo. Please get into my body and live as my flesh.* When Soonboon brought her tongue to the ground, his mouth twisted into a wicked smile. She chewed dirt in her mouth. Her mouth was filled with the wet smell of dirt. Just then, his subordinate ran to him hurriedly and saluted.

"You should go to the commander's office. You have a telegram."

He went off to the commander's office urgently after hearing these words. Soonboon lay down on the ground when he left. The girls immediately vomited all their food, holding onto their stomachs as he walked away.

Soonboon couldn't cry. Kumok remained quiet as if none of it was believable.

I should have died with Bongnyeo.

35. Plan for Revenge

The sun tapped Soonboon's face as she lay down like she had fainted. Her unwashed face was roughly exposed in the light. Soonboon liked the sunshine. She felt like her body became light and floated when she gave herself to the sunshine. Wings unfolded from her armpits and opened quietly in the sun, carried by the wind. Soonboon followed the sun by moving her body whenever it moved. As soldiers came into her room, she served them with her eyes shut tight.

Strangely, she felt free and comfortable. She didn't need to worry about anything and didn't need to fear anything.

The body is only a shell, they will never violate my pure spirit, I am Soonboon always. Kim, Soonboon. A daughter of Korea and a woman of Korea: Kim, Soonboon. Break my soul if you can, I will be reborn as Kim, Soonboon.

She didn't go out for breakfast even when the bell clang for distribution. Kumok shared hers each time.

"Again today? You didn't get a meal today, again?" Kumok entered Soonboon's room holding a rice ball.

"How will you keep going like this? Please eat some."

Kumok split her rice ball in half and gave it to Soonboon, but she shut her mouth firmly and turned her head aside; she smelled Bongnyeo on every piece of food. It smelled like Bongnyeo in the water, in the rice ball, and even in the air. Bongnyeo's smell was stagnant and soaked into everything. She might not be able to escape from her smell, even in death.

"Why don't you eat? Do you want to die? Do you really want to die like this?" Kumok urged her, begging. But Soonboon didn't budge an inch.

"Are you doing this because of Bongnyeo? Right? She said you should survive and not die. She died to save you. So, what would she say if she saw you doing this? She would not want you to live like this."

Soonboon shut her eyes again when Kumok mentioned Bongnyeo. She felt nauseous again.

"Be alive, live. Stay alive for Bongnyeo. We don't know what will happen in the future, but we need to survive until then."

Soonboon tried to raise her upper body, but she sat back down on the floor as the world twirled and filled with spots.

"Soonboon, Soonboon," Kumok shook her shoulder. Soonboon felt even more nauseous as Kumok shook her.

"You'll be dead if you stay like this. You know how they treat sick girls, so please, eat and save your energy."

Soonboon knew that they didn't need sick girls, so they treated them even worse. Once they were sick, they took the girls away, that was the end. They knew that the girls would never come back although they didn't ask what happened to them, or nobody talked about it. Soonboon could end up the same.

"Get up, please. How can I live if you die? Please get up for me, please... I am sad because you are always thinking about only Bongnyeo. You are the same as my family. I have only you. How can I survive without you?" Soonboon looked at Kumok carefully as she spoke. Her face was yellow.

"I can't live without you, please..."

Kumok's eyes were getting gradually wet. After listening to Kumok's complain, Soonboon suddenly thought that she had committed a sin.

Kumok is right, I need to survive for Bongnyeo. She rolled over the nail board to save my life, so I should not waste her sacrifice. Indeed, I should not die like this.

Soonboon thought that she could survive even if they tried to kill her. She should survive for Bongnyeo and Kumok.

I will accuse them after I survive. I will speak out to the world about their brutality and cruelty. However, if I really wish to die, I will kill Kanemura first.

"I am fine, I will get back on my feet. Sure, I will." Soonboon gathered all her energy from below her belly button and got up. Kumok's face brightened right away seeing Soonboon get up.

"Okay, sure, you should."

Kumok poured some water into a bowl and handed it to Soonboon. She brought the bowl to her mouth. There was Bongnyeo's smell coming from the water. *Barf!* Kumok grimaced as Soonboon retched.

"I will die if you die," Kumok said resolutely.

"Why are you dying? You need to survive until the end. You said I should survive. Don't worry, I will not die," Soonboon said.

"Are you sure? Really? I can't live without you. I can't live by myself if you die."

"Why are you feeling alone? Other girls are here."

"Maybe, but, but, they aren't like you and Bongnyeo…"

"Don't say that," Soonboon tried to persuade her, but she had the same thought.

Then let's eat. Okay. Let's eat for Kumok. Soonboon drank a sip of water once and then again, and let it flow into her body. Kumok patted Soonboon's back while she looked at her.

Bongnyeo, please, allow me to worry about Kumok, and please forgive me. Forgive me for Kumok, Soonboon said as if she whispered to Bongnyeo. She brought the rice ball into her mouth little by little. The rough feeling of cooked barley scratched her esophagus, but she swallowed it down with her saliva. She swallowed and swallowed over and over. If she kept going, she might swallow life, death, and her life up to this point as an animal. Then she might be indifferent about everything someday.

"Thank you for eating. I really appreciate it."

Soonboon felt sisterly affection in Kumok's tone. She just nodded. *Right, it's better for me to live like this. Let's figure out what exists at the end of this road. I need to find out what exists at the end of the path for Bongnyeo.* Soonboon comforted herself. Kumok made sure Soonboon finished her portion, then she ate the leftovers.

The sun is so bright. It grows living things. Living things store the sunshine in their bodies, then are filled with the promise of the next life. If they don't keep growing, they won't produce any fruit, and life ends. Fruits are the energy of the sunshine and a promise of the next life. They lead their lives with meaning, whether they live well or just keep living since they are not dead.

36. Chosenpi[5]

The girls' rooms lost their inhabitants one by one, but they weren't emptied for long. One day, all of a sudden, the rooms were filled with new girls and the rooms were shaken again by new humiliation and assaults. Nobody could remember how many girls were dead and how many were now forgotten from their memories. Their names, their faces, everything floated around like a rumor, like a lost memory in the chilly wind.

'Chosenpi.'

They called themselves that now. Opium made Kumok more helpless day by day. Yes, their lives were hard to tolerate. It was the same whether they died this way or the other way. If they could forget their animal-like lives for a moment, it was thanks to the opium. The girls all withstood their lives in the comfort station in their own ways.

Soldiers continued to visit the girls regularly. They smelled more and more profoundly of death. The scent came from their uniforms, from their mouths, and from their bleary eyes. The smell of death permeated everything. Death revealed itself through the smell of blood and gunpowder. The musty, morbid scents gradually tightened around their necks. The smell of death grew thicker and stronger every day.

Soonboon and the other girls now needed to go to the battlefield by truck to comfort the soldiers there. Soldiers took out their penises and lunged at them, screwed up by the dust in the trenches. The girls were scared of the soldiers' red eyes, but there was no place to run away at the trenches. The long

---

[5] Japanese slang, which means "Korean comfort women."

holes looked like graveyards, graveyards they made for themselves while they were still alive.

The soldiers had spent their early lives as murderers and would meet their deaths in the trenches at last. They were obsessed with the girls more in the trenches than in the comfort station. They were like dogs, like disgusting animals. Soonboon's back was scratched, her skin peeled back, but they didn't care. Her pain didn't have any meaning in the face of their own deaths. Some of the men cried during intercourse. Everyone was afraid of death as it approached them closely. Or maybe it was anger. Perhaps they were angry about dying so young.

Soonboon felt much more pain in her genitals on the day when she came back from the battlefield.

37. Kumok is Sick

Hail-like rain poured and stuck to the ground. It was torrential. The ground shook with the sound of the raindrops. Especially today, lots of soldiers were waiting for their turns in front of the girls' rooms due to the rain. Soonboon didn't get any breaks that day. She was also delirious from yesterday's injection. That might have been the reason why she felt the sound of rain was so sad. It started at noon and dropped on and off repeatedly. *What are mom and dad doing now? Did the balsam flowers that dad sprinkled grow well and sow seeds?* Each time it rained, thoughts of home circled in her mind.

Knock, knock. Kumok didn't come out from her room. Soonboon knocked again, thinking maybe she missed the signal because of the sound of the rain. *Knock, knock,* still no response. When Soonboon tried to turn, and lay down, the answer came: *knock, knock.*

It was Kumok. Soonboon responded right away, gladly. *Knock, knock.* Soonboon went over to Kumok's room quickly.

"I am here," Soonboon said.

"Yes."

Kumok's response was inattentive, her face somehow strange in the candlelight.

"Are you sick?" Soonboon asked with a face full of worry. She was concerned about Kumok a lot recently.

"No." Kumok shook her head, but her shaking looked different than usual. Her eyes seemed to have lost their focus and were sleepy.

"Did you take opium again?" Soonboon asked, upset.

"No, what opium?" Kumok trailed off.

"What are you going to do?"

"I am fine, I am really fine, don't worry about me," Kumok mumbled.

"How can I not be worried about you? Please, get real."

Kumok shut her mouth and Soonboon continued to worry.

"Please quit the opium from now on, try to stop. It is stupid to use drugs, it's crazy."

"I couldn't stand it here. I can't live without it," Kumok answered, losing her confidence.

"But how can you take opium, knowing it harms your body?"

"I feel like I am going to die if I don't have it."

"I don't want to lose you, try to withstand it. Hang in there."

Kumok mumbled again: "That asshole... Kanemura, that son of bitch..."

Kumok shut her mouth as she tried to say something. Soonboon knew that Kanemura had injected opium into girls. He made them weak so he could ravish them whenever he wanted. He probably did it to Kumok too. He didn't only inject the opium into the girls; he used it on the soldiers to improve their fighting power; to remove their fears. He used the drug on the soldiers to make them fight like they were crazy in the rain of bullets on the battlefield.

Kumok's shoulders shook slightly. Soonboon didn't argue with her anymore. They just listened to the sound of the rain as they sat side by side. *Dot a dot dot, dot a dot dot,* it sounded like corn popping in a popcorn machine. The sound aroused great sorrow in the two girls who had lost their way in the middle of their young lives.

"Did you like that soldier?" Kumok asked unexpectedly after listening to the sound of the rain for a while.

"Who?"

"The Korean soldier."

Soonboon realized right away who Kumok was talking about- the Korean soldier who would stay calm when he came to her or left after only sleeping for a while. After he would leave, a bag of cookies and military tickets were left behind.

"What do you mean if I like him?" Soonboon tried to ask, 'How could I like him with this dirty body?' but stopped.

"If he asks to run away, go with him, don't stay here."

"Where could I run away?"

"If you can, go with him."

Soonboon looked at Kumok. *Where would I go if I could?* There was no place to go, she didn't know where. Or rather, she was more afraid of life after escaping the comfort station.

"He seems to like you, so go with him if he wants to run away."

"How could I dare to like him?" "No, it would be fine if he really likes you, do follow him."

"What about you?"

"I..." Kumok didn't finish her words.

"I won't go, I won't go anywhere without you. Bongnyeo would want the same thing."

Just then, there was a scream from a girl's room. The screaming mixed with the sound of rain was amplified in the night. Kumok covered her ears with both hands and dug her face between her knees. That night, the scream mixed with rain was horrific, and it didn't stop. *Ahh...it hurts.*

Kumok was perplexed, breathing deeply as the screaming continued. Soonboon hugged her and patted her back.

"It's okay, it's fine, it'll get better soon..." Soonboon said rhythmically, like a song that her mom would sing while stroking her aching tummy.

"It's okay, it's fine, it'll be alright..."

However, Kumok shook her head sharply, blocking her ears with both hands more firmly. *Ahhh! Ahhh!* The sound continued; it never stopped.

"It's okay, it's fine, it'll be alright..."

"It's okay, it's fine, it'll..."

38. Farewell, Kumok

Nobody talked about how the war was going. During this time, the siren wailed more often, and the soldiers didn't come back from the battlefield for many days.

The Korean soldier who always visited Soonboon didn't come to Soonboon's room anymore. She didn't know whether he was alive or dead. Strangely, Soonboon felt an emptiness like a part of her heart was cut off. The empty space he left behind was bigger than she thought. *No, I should not, no, I can't*, she kept denying it, but she liked him very much. She shouldn't have this feeling. Moreover, shouldn't love him. Bad person...She was embarrassed about her feelings; how could she love one of these men, how could she have this feeling with her dirty body?

There is no spring in this country, there is no fall or winter either: there is only one season. Exciting changes of seasons where the scenery transformed and the colors of leaves and flowers didn't happen in this country. Although the weather was always hot, Soonboon's heart had turned cold.

It was extremely hot that day. When Soonboon swept the dust from the *tatami*, wiping the beads of sweat from her forehead, a girl's scream came from Kumok's room. Soonboon stood up and jumped like a metal spring, and ran to her room. What happened? What's wrong? Kumok was sleeping quietly, it seemed she slept without dreaming. Why? What's wrong? Soonboon asked with her eyes. The girl who shook the morning heat in the comfort station pointed at Kumok with her eyes. She was peacefully asleep, why? Soonboon asked her with her eyes again. But the girl looking at Kumok kept pointing at her. Soonboon approached Kumok. Something unknown, and her very peaceful expression weighed down on Soonboon. Just then, Soonboon saw some blood clogged on her wrist. Blood flashed through Soonboon's mind and then passed.

One day, Kumok had said that the girl who had stayed in her room previously had killed herself by slitting her wrist after having opium and had sucked her own blood. Kumok's words still rang in her ears. No, no, no way...

"Kumok!"

Soonboon burst into tears as she clutched Kumok. No, she didn't have any tears at the start because just couldn't believe it, didn't want to believe it, so she just kept holding Kumok.

"Kumok!" Soonboon's call came back to her as an echo after bouncing around the room. The girls gathered around hesitantly when they heard her screaming. *Don't die, please don't die. How can I live if you die? How can I live without you?* She felt like Kumok spoke to her with the same words Kumok had begged her with when Bongnyeo died.

"But, what about... what about me? How can I live without you? Whom can I depend on now?" Her heart was broken, she couldn't talk, she couldn't move, she couldn't think anything...

What about me? How can I live without you? Whom can I depend on now?

She kept asking these questions to herself. No answers came.

Kumok left carried in a handcart, the same as the other dead girls. Only those who carried her knew where she was being sent. Soonboon sat down on the floor as they took her away. All her power slipped away in a moment. Now, it was her turn. It was her turn now that she had lost Bongnyeo and Kumok.

Okay, I will follow you soon. Farewell, Kumok! Don't feel pain anymore, don't suffer there. Be well with Bongnyeo. Let's comfort ourselves knowing we were once born in the world, though we died after living shameful lives, having been born at the wrong time.

Although my life means less than that of an animal, you and Bongnyeo gave me such comfort in my life. Therefore, your short lifetime was not meaningless, it was a great life only by itself. Goodbye, Kumok! I will miss that place where you are now.

Soonboon sat there, emptying herself. She lost all hope after Kumok was sent off like that, in vain. She lost the hope of going back home alive.

Life was meaningless now. She could die anytime if she made up her mind to do it. She could run away anytime to follow Kumok and Bongnyeo, and escape from this world as they had. *Catch me if you can, never, I will never be caught.*

39. Nightmare Recommenced

Days and months passed. Time passed inattentively though the world was going crazy. Soonboon was lonely living without Kumok and Bongnyeo. She felt like a part of her heart was empty, and the passing of time made her powerless. Soonboon wished only to die by cutting her remaining time bit by bit. No, she didn't want to die by herself. She wanted to take the cruel man, Kanemura, to Bongnyeo and Kumok. She was waiting for her chance, for him to come. She decided over and over that she would kill him when he came to her.

But for one thing, she was worried about the remaining girls. They would continue to be cruelly harassed, and be punished instead of her. This guilt weighed heavily on her, so she delayed the action each time.

Then one day, the meal distribution bell didn't ring though the time to eat had already passed. In the meantime, the sun shone deeply into the girls' rooms. They gathered around the meal distribution area one by one, feeling that something was off. They didn't see any soldiers. Neither guards nor surveillance was to be seen. The truck that came on and off the military station was nowhere, and no soldiers could be seen, either. What happened? What's wrong? The girls asked each other with their eyes, but they shook their heads. I don't know, I don't know, either. They talked to each other with embarrassed expressions.

Just then, a girl shouted:

"Run away, escape this place quickly! Japan lost the war! They are coming to kill us, so hurry!" she shouted as she ran toward the forest. The other girls followed her, screaming and running into the woods. Soonboon followed them, running to not be separated from them. Her heart was pounding. The war was over. Japan had lost the war.

The girls climbed the mountain in a group. Nobody knew where they were, they just ran in confusion. When girls asked her how she knew, the shouting girl answered, "A Burman who delivered supplies to the troops notified me to run away as soon as possible. Japan lost the war and they are coming to kill us. They are coming to remove all evidence of us." These words made their skin crawl. They ran up the mountain one after the other, still not knowing their way around, but they couldn't stop though they slipped and fell.

The forest didn't hide them, they ran away desperately, but then suddenly a group of soldiers blocked them. The girls were too afraid to say anything. But these were not the Japanese soldiers whom the girls had seen every day. They were tall, with big noses, and didn't speak Japanese, either. They were Americans. One of the soldiers asked, "Who are you?" But nobody understood what he said; the girls just looked at him full of fear. The Burman beside him said something as he looked at the girls. The American soldier looked up and down the girls while speaking in his language that they didn't understand. They made the girls walk ahead of them, back to the military station.

The Imperial Japanese Army who had assured victory in this holy war had entirely vanished, and the base was deserted. The barbed wire sat hideous in the empty space. It was no longer the same barbed wire as yesterday. It was not the stubborn, arrogant wire that had divided the world into sides, and oppressed their freedom. It had lost its absolute power. Looking closely now some parts of it were broken down by red rust. They hadn't noticed this until now.

Soonboon and the girls waited for a few days. They walked around and took the sunshine in through their whole bodies, they watched the sunset, looked at the birds returning to their nests, and then fell asleep. But their freedom was uncomfortable and apprehensive for them, so they suddenly would wake up and look around aimlessly in the middle of the night.

Once everything was settled down, they would be allowed to go back to home. The girls were unfamiliar with and afraid of this sudden freedom. What would they do? They were all nervous.

"Are you going to go back to your hometown?"

Soonboon shook her head quietly and resolutely when a girl asked her this. Some wanted to go back to their homes, others didn't just like Soonboon.

She wished to go, but she couldn't. She had missed and missed again the house that had bloomed with the red balsam flowers her dad had planted. She missed her mom's warm touch and father's quiet smile… but she couldn't go back there. The place where mom plucked out the grass with tough hands and dad tilled the land with a sunbaked face. She couldn't go back there no matter how much she missed them.

I will lead my life by wandering around, anywhere. I will live like a floating, shaking flower petal on the water.

Soonboon decided to throw away what remained of her life, which had already been torn down into pieces, a life that had been ruined totally. Therefore, what remained of her life was not to be lived but to be thrown away. Since she had not lived as a person, how could she live what was left as such? Thus, she made up her mind to wander in unfamiliar places with different names until her life would end. She would go to places where nobody knew her and nobody remembered her.

Soonboon knew how hard life could be for a woman who had been plucked from her roots. Her life was solely her responsibility and her own burden to bear from now on. *Do you see me, Bongnyeo and Kumok? I was able to withstand it because of you. I wish I could be with you. Where are you girls now?*

Soonboon came out of the comfort station and walked down the road without anyone preventing her. Nobody stopped her, not a man, a gun, or a siren either.

The sun was shining splendidly on the road, the world faded white by the sunlight. She inhaled deeply. It was a different air from what she had breathed in a long time. The sun absorbed into all of her blood as she breathed the unfamiliar air. She needed to go somewhere else. Wherever she went, she would be able to control her life again. The weight of life started to bear down on her heavily. Life might be tough by herself.

Soonboon made a fan with her hands and looked up at the sky. *Where should I go? Where can I go?* Soonboon was standing in the middle of the road. *Where are you, butterfly? Butterfly, please come here...*

Butterfly, take me wherever you go. Let's float around the world together, let's roam this world while missing my mom, my dad, and the balsam flowers under the fence. Let's wander the world and throw our lives to the wind, together.

Soonboon walked along the road. The winding road lay down, stark white under the dazzling sunshine.

• • •

Contributors for publishing this book: Samuel Lee, Jintae Lee, Mihee Eun, Sahyun Youn, Jae-Yang Park, Daehwan Kim, Sangho Chung, Namsik Kim, Jin-San Yoo, Ghmseop Yang, Seungsu Yang, Sujeong Park, Sang Hwa Lee, Haekang Jang, Hojae Ahn, Harry Lee, Jason Park, Jaesik Choi, Alexander Son, Keumjoo Lee, Woogeun Eun, Yongwoo Lee, Cheongah Kim, Sangho Lee, Myungku Choi, Jegook Lee, Bunim Kim, Unyun Kim, Kyung Chung, Ju-hyun Song, Hyeon-ju Kim, Hyojin Kim, Dongbaek Lee, Wonseok Jeong, Dukman Kim, Seolmi Kim, Yenkang Sunim, Kim Crandall, Dongha Lee, Kwan Nam, Sunki Kim, Jiin Hong, Cheongwoo Lee, Sangyi Lee, You Chan Jeong, Hyunfung Chang, Sang Won Lee, Kihwan Lee, Jinwook Joo, Ally C. Choi, Jeong-Soo Choe, Dongwoo Kim, Ghejung Cho, Sangjun Park, Junghee Shin, MiSeon Hooper, William Won-Bok Lee, Junghwan Kim, Yoo-Hyun Daniel Sung, Sungmin Kim, Chulmin Kim, Chungju Lee, Kelly Hooper, Unje Kim, Jungki Kim, Youngsin Kim, Munjin Park, Jaehee Hong, Seung-e You, Dong-Hyeon Yun, Yeonhee Jang, Sungyong Youn, Sunyi Kang, Miwon Pae, Eunjun Lee, Heesook An, Eunsook An, Youngsook An, Yongho Chi, Yeonsil Kim, Brittany Benson, and several anonymous donors.

Please visit https://www.facebook.com/groups/FlutterFlutterButterfly/

CPSIA information can be obtained
at www.ICGtesting.com
Printed in the USA
LVHW02s1600140218
566600LV00011B/790/P